SPARSELY ATTENDED FUNERALS

by Mark Wilson

Close To The Bone Publishing

<u>Work previously published</u>

we never shit – first published in *Rejection Letters*

yakee candle impotence – first published in *Misery Tourism*

for family

CONTENTS

SPARSELY ATTENDED FUNERALS

WE NEVER SHIT

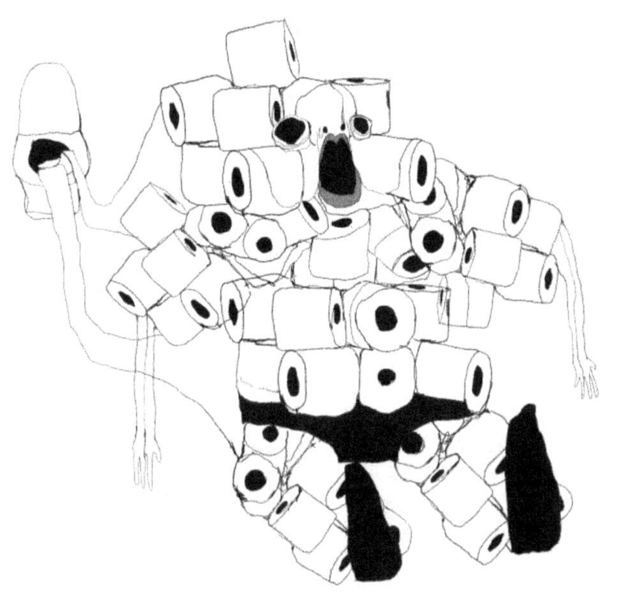

We hated watching it shit so we removed its asshole. We hated the way it breathed so we removed its mouth. We were sick of it listening so we removed its ears. We were sick of it watching so we removed its eyes.

We were left with the most adorable living adjacent dog anyone could want. A ball of fur and limbs wandering aimlessly for us to stroke and save our marriage.

We too eventually got the surgeries, a house of smooth unblemished flesh, finally living peacefully.

People loved us for that.

YANKEE CANDLE
IMPOTENCE

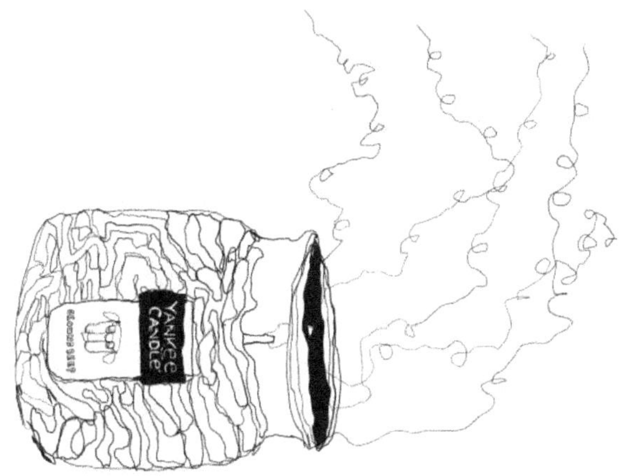

I was depressed and one Saturday got drunk enough to drive to the Yankee Candle nestled in the strip mall on Grape Road. It was right next to a restaurant that allowed customers to throw peanuts on the ground, a mundane ritual that was celebrated as some transcendent act of charity and recounted with reverence to anyone who would listen. I thought about the janitor sometimes and how they had to sweep up the spit and peanut threads and wondered how difficult it was to scoop the happiness of a town into an old dustpan that management refused to replace.

I never really cared for candles, but when the drink tells you go somewhere you fucking go somewhere. So I guess I was going to buy a candle or worst case scenario sell my piss-stained khakis to some goddamn loser at Plato's Closet who was into that type of thing. Sometimes I'd spend hours peering into the strip mall shop windows, hoping that soon enough their windows would be boarded up like everything eventually was.

Something about the parasitic relationship of the city and we who lived there was comforting: inconveniences to each other that coexisted against our respective wills. The city, a pile of shit incapable of swatting the flies that chose it as home. Us as flies picking at the malnourished bowel movement until eventually exhausting ourselves and dying in its warm embrace.

The drive was fine and I stayed mostly on the road. I furiously smoked a handful of cigarette filters and felt the white hairs grow a few more inches on my swollen tongue. I felt the saliva moving slowly through a jigsaw of bacteria, probing every crack on its way to a jacuzzi of bile and whiskey.

The store was as magnificent as the drink had told me. With a drywall facade like you wouldn't believe and even some stickers on the windows advertising deals. I became mildly aroused and began to cry at the sight of the thing sitting behind a dirty mound of snow in my hometown. I don't believe in fate, but if I did, I'd say my wholly forgettable life had brought me here for salvation, a lifeline from a city that had held my head in stagnant waters of its polluted river for decades.

The inside was empty, save a pear-shaped employee who was fondling a candle in the back, barely distinguishable to the naked eye. It smelled like a microwaved cotton candy pumpkin and I felt the scent crawl slowly down my throat with my post nasal. The smell of raw onions followed along with the perspiration of indistinguishable spit meat.

"Welcome to Yankee Candle!" he yelled abruptly, painfully waddling over to where I stood.

"Thanks," I replied listlessly.

"I know why you're here today," he said, licking a sizable dead skin chunk from his bleeding upper lip.

Was this portly man my savior? Were his sausage fingers to fix all of my problems? He seemed oddly aware of the disrepair I existed in. Poor and lonely, eternally drunk, filled with vague regret. I began to cry again and almost hugged him, ready for the wisdom he would undoubtedly share.

"All of our candles are now fuckable," he said pridefully, wringing his wet heads hard enough for a liquid to drip visibly onto the already soiled carpet.

I watched him pick up a hulking bastard of a candle that was scented like ground beef and spin it around to reveal a crudely carved hole at the base of it. He looked up at me gleaming, his eyes filling with the same tears as mine, his pit stains growing darker yet. I could hear his teeth grinding in the quiet shop; he looked like a proud parent at their son's first Little League game, except instead of a childhood dream it was a fuckable candle.

I didn't ask too many questions, as a confrontation with a candle that oozed carnal urge was unexpected. I shakily extracted my wallet and paid the man for the candle in expired coupons and lugged it out to my car. He waved at me through the glass, offering a coy wink and a smile that seemed like a corporate mandate.

After a few months, every fiber in my piece of shit apartment smelled like synthetic ground beef and I fell in love with the candle. When the last piece of wax fell to my carpet, I knew I had to return to the shop and the man that had saved my life with his glory hole candle.

When I went into the shop a new employee stood smugly at the door.

"Can I help you sir?" he asked.

"I'm looking for a pear-shaped bastard, very sweaty, think his name was Nick," I replied.

"No one here by that name, can I interest you in our new hard boiled egg candle? All the egg smell none of the egg hell,"

Damnit he was really playing hardball, he was going to make me ask for the fuckable ground beef candle, make me admit how pathetic I was at a strip mall candle store, melt me into wax and reshape me into a candle that smelled like a petting zoo.

I asked him and he told me that Yankee Candle does not condone candle modifications, like he was reading out of some bullshit candle bible or PSA on the mistreatment of candles. I told him I understood and purchased a grass clippings candle to diffuse the awkwardness. He waved and winked at me just like Nick did, but this guy was no connoisseur.

Later I sat at home drunk again, reflecting on my newly found impotence to the scent of freshly mowed grass and devising a plan for hunting down the stranger in the store that had given me a taste of that forbidden fruit. Months later, I drove by the strip mall and found the windows boarded up, this time the failure wasn't comforting.

The plywood suggested I would never find him again, the emptiness implied I would never fuck another candle.

THE RUST BELT BLED DONKEY SAUCE

The donkey sauce was killing us. Either that or the factories that produced nothing in particular and impregnated the clouds and air with sulfur and asbestos, maybe it was a combination, whatever the case, my handkerchiefs were filling with more blood every week and my bones could barely hold my sagging flesh as it plummeted toward the worn asphalt of the strip mall I worked at. Flavortown bordered Gary in Northern Indiana and was an unassuming settlement that my friends and I had moved to ironically five years back in an effort to generate social media content for uninterested friends and family.

The content was generated, consumed, and shit out with an expired batch of Guy-talian Fondue Dippers and now we were all stuck here in the same toilet. We didn't check the fine print on our lease, which included a mandatory decade long service with a death penalty clause if breached. We had seen someone try to leave Flavortown before their time was up; the next day there was a public hanging during an Imagine Dragons concert.

Much like Gary, Flavortown was the beating heart of directionless pollution as its web of veins and arteries poisoned surrounding cities in the already deteriorating rust belt. Our jobs were to extract the donkey sauce from the donkeys themselves. Though I didn't really consider them donkeys at all. They were human donkey hybrids, the lab creation of some truly awful bastard. I figured there was an easier way to get thousand island dressing mixed with ranch, but we were told that milking the skin tagged utters of these neglected donkeys that looked vaguely like Guy Fieri was the only true way to provide the American public with what they wanted. They didn't seem to mind much, indifferent to the condiment their bodies generated, they were hooked to televisions that broadcasted Diners, Drive-Ins and Dives and were fed DMT regularly. In some ways, I wished I was them and in other ways I felt us becoming more similar by the day.

I'd once hatched a plot to escape, thinking I could ride one of the creatures to freedom. Thinking that I could save us both from the town that was grinding us like peppercorn into drool filled tourist mouths as their tongues probed the ears of unsuspecting servers. Thinking that its atrophied legs would somehow be more capable than mine, able to outrun imminent death in favor of the prolonged one everyone else seemed to enjoy.

When I hopped on, ready for salvation, the last thing I heard was bones snapping before its legs crumpled completely and we both collapsed into the asphalt. That was the last time I tried to leave and the death of something so innocent only functioned to spiral me deeper into the depression that accompanied existing for the sole purpose of condiment accumulation and passive organ rotting from pollution.

Now I got drunk and hoped things would change without a catalyst. Assuming that things would just work themselves out, even though I knew they wouldn't.

We'd all die here. We'd be buried in flame decal button up shirts and backwards upside down sunglasses like everyone else who had died harvesting the sauce. At least we had provided the secret dressing that lubricated the esophagi of dying Americans enough to consume another fistful of knuckle steak at airport bar and grills across the country; at least we had done that.

SIX FLAGS GREAT AMERICA AND THE AFTERLIFE

Six Flags Great America in Gurnee, Illinois, was a place dreams were made of. At least for those of us lucky enough to dream. And I guess it wasn't the entire city. Actually, Six Flags seemed to exist as a city in itself. A fucking deep-fried utopia that transcended society itself. I dream quite a bit myself, but they're mostly awful, unlike colossal steel gods that effortlessly hoisted screaming inbred losers into the sky before plummeting them back down to earth. I was one of those losers. I bought a season pass every year because nowhere else felt much like home. My life would be a whole lot better off if I had woken up to the smell of funnel cakes and dandruff instead of low-fat Greek yogurt. I can't remember when I started buying season passes, in fact, I don't recall a lot from outside of the park.

Either way, the invention of the season pass is up there with some of the greatest inventions in human history. Nothing else had a more significant impact on me. Some people cried looking at art; I cried looking at a stucco carnival entrance in Gurnee.

Pollock wished he could paint something as beautiful as the third loop on Tatsu. Most artists aren't worth a damn anyway, but I resent that pieces of shit like Pollock are celebrated over the engineers of something so pure.

Any stuffy bastard aimlessly dragging his club feet across a polished museum floor is no more or less cultured than the guy in jean shorts sticking his dick into a freshly bought cup of Dippin' Dots. I would actually argue that the latter is more able to comprehend true beauty. His understanding of the world wasn't dictated to him through books or peers. In fact, he probably couldn't read. He is under no burden of conformity or judgment and can enjoy things without some godforsaken standard, because he has none. He just knows that the cold feels good on his junk in the heat and there is beauty in that too.

Maybe they picked Gurnee for the contrast of beauty and despair. That something so incredible could exist in such a piece of shit city. Maybe it was for taxes, or maybe it was because they wanted to give something to somewhere that had nothing else. I guess it was likely a combination of the three, but I've never bothered to look it up. Anyways, that was back then. Six Flags now is something entirely different. My dad used to tell me about the wooden roller coasters, even about the transition from wood to steel. That excited a lot of people, but there was constantly a longing for something more. I guess there always is, at least when it applies to amusement parks.

My dad actually died a few years back of dementia. Or I guess of other things caused by dementia. The one thing he remembered was those roller coasters. We'd talk about them whenever I visited him in the hospital and when he felt like talking. Most of the time, he didn't. Either way, I hope at least he was thinking about them, though I guess I wasn't sure if he could still think. Sometimes we stared at the TV for hours and I would glance over to see if he was still awake, which he always was. A few years of this and he was gone. I was ungodly sad after it happened and actually couldn't do much for the better part of a decade. I didn't do a lot before it either, I guess, but after, I really did nothing.

At this point in my life, I couldn't even afford a season pass, so I mostly masturbated and slept. I wasn't a big drinker, but if I were, you could bet I would have been shit-faced. Even drinking took energy – energy I didn't have. My speech at the funeral was shit, by the way. I spent weeks writing and then froze completely in the moment and ended up just sniveling like an insect. No one really blamed me, but I couldn't help feeling like the biggest asshole to ever live. I posted the whole thing on Instagram a few days later and got eleven sympathy likes. Maybe it wasn't as bad as I thought.

I worked some odd jobs and got fired. I got fired at an Auntie Anne's in the airport for trading a sack of pretzels for a Wahlburger. In my exit interview, my manager told me he'd rather eat a bag of dicks than a Wahlburger and I didn't really understand the hatred. The burger was alright. Years later, I found out that the manager of Wahlburgers had fucked my manager's wife, so I guess I was just a casualty of cuckolding. I was broke as fuck for a while. I collected my unemployment, but I needed a way to buy the damn season pass to Six Flags because that was the only place where I was remotely happy.

One time, I watched *Maury* on daytime television and saw a commercial for a class-action lawsuit against the nursing home I had put my dad in. Apparently, it was a notorious goddamn hot-spot for elderly neglect and such, so I called the number and explained how he had died recently. I didn't want to profit off of his death, but what else was there to do? I'm not sure what happened next, but after a few months, my lawyer said I would be paid $1.2 million by the insurance company of the nursing home. I celebrated like hell that day. I guess I was happier than the guy who just found out he wasn't the father of three kids on *Maury*. I wondered how the kids would feel years later watching this, or how they even felt now. Knowing that someone was celebrating the opportunity to have nothing to do with them. I guess they would keep looking until they found someone who wanted to be there or was indifferent, at least. I didn't let it dampen my mood too much, but it was kind of fucked up to think about.

For all of those years I didn't go to the Six Flags, they were working on some top-secret ride. Well, they described it as "much more than just a ride," but no one was really sure what that meant. They had a whole mysterious marketing campaign behind it, probably the most protracted marketing campaign ever. Ten years of marketing something that didn't even exist, I wondered how fucking miserable the meetings were that kept cranking out the self-indulgent bullshit commercials. I still loved the park more than anything, but goddammit, I hated those commercials. There was one where Carson Daly was baptized by Ryan Seacrest, while Josh Groban played *On Angels Wings*.

Everyone was naked too, which seemed weird, but it kind of fit the vaguely religious undertone of them all. Another commercial was a matte black cross that flashed across the screen for 40 seconds, eventually having to pull it because of seizures.

On Twitter and Instagram, everyone was posting about this part of the park that was roped off. The one thing they couldn't hide was a tarp extending into the sky. Whatever was underneath that cover must have been one big bastard. At a certain point, it was lost in the clouds. The strange part was it didn't really look like anyone was ever working on it, but I guess they were because the thing kept growing. I wondered for years what masterpiece was underneath it.

The day I received my settlement check, I drove my car to the park. It was only about a twenty-minute drive from Mundelein, where I regrettably lived. I ended up there because that was where my mom lived and after my dad died, she wasn't doing too great. Though neither was I, so it really made sense for us to not be great together. My therapist would argue otherwise, but fuck him, what did he know? He warned against squandering my life as a caretaker without really taking care of myself and had some insane theory about a cycle of negative thinking, but I could mourn my dad as long as I wanted. Who's to say what too much or too little mourning is? Plus, it was a free place to stay.

Anyways, when I got to the park, the line to get in was pretty damn long. Actually, the longest I've ever seen it. When I got close to the kiosk, I saw an advertisement for the new attraction, a black poster with the word 'Afterlife' written on it. It looked pretty fucking stupid in all actuality, way too dramatic for my liking. It didn't fit, something seemed off about it. I put my money on the counter and told the lady I wanted a season pass. She said they were selling a new package that included a VIP 'Afterlife' experience. I told her to get fucked and take her shit somewhere else, I just wanted to ride Goliath and maybe get this year's commemorative sun visor. I wanted to remember my dad. She said she would sell me a season pass but gave me a brochure about the new attraction, which was apparently opening the following week.

I took the brochure figuring I would use it as a napkin later because, at the time, I considered myself somewhat of an environmentalist. This mainly involved sometimes recycling things when convenient and refilling my soap bottles with water. My activism was fueled by cheapness more than anything else. I liked trees and all, but I guess me cutting my soap with water wasn't really saving any rainforests.

I stayed at the park from open to close and rode everything I wanted to ride, a welcome first as the lines were incredibly sparse. Sometimes it seemed like I was the only person in the park. I left the park sunburned and having to shit really bad, feeling complete and utter happiness. The enormous cherry Coke and buffet of indistinguishable deep-fried nuggets were borrowed commodities that needed to be paid into the nearest bathroom. Usually, that meant the park bathroom, but fortunately, my house was only 20 minutes away, so I figured I could make it. It was worth holding if I could. That was always the risk, but I wasn't wearing my favorite boxers or anything, so I figured what the hell. I had a few bad experiences in the bathrooms at the Six Flags, one of which included the stall resident next to me having the big one. I didn't know it was a heart attack at the time, but when I saw him clutching his chest and crawling his way under my stall, I figured something was wrong.

I dialed 911 like anyone would, but he ended up dying regardless. I wasn't sure how often it happened and the EMT told me, "You'd be surprised." I wouldn't prefer dying that way, but hell, some of these people had to expect it. Passing a day's worth of deep-fried Snickers and Mountain Dew Code Red dipped corn dogs isn't as easy as it looks. Part of me wondered if these stalls were their noose and the snack foods, the gust of wind that would knock the chair out from under their feet that had perched dubiously on the edge for all of those years.

I made it back to the house to shit, but barely. I waved at my mom and then pointed to my ass before running serpentine upstairs to dump all the park had to offer into our modest toilet. While I was sitting there, I saw the brochure sticking limply from the front pocket of my jeans and I decided to read it because I was sick of all of my friends on Instagram, which had turned into a group of like-minded people resentfully liking each other's brutal posturing and curating. Everyone seemed to hate each other as much as the pornstars I masturbated to, but much like them, they continued to suck and fuck. I guess it was more routine than anything else or whatever.

I opened the brochure even though the pages were kind of stuck together. I pulled gently on each side and finally tore the stubborn bastards from each other and took a glimpse inside.

Jesus Christ, you wouldn't believe what I saw. General admission tickets were $500,000 and VIP access was— you guessed it, $1.2 million. What kind of sick fuck determined this pricing? What could be worth THAT much money? This was an amusement park heresy! Also, I was getting paranoid at how the VIP package was the exact same price as my settlement, but either way, it was probably just some cost-benefit analysis or something. Fucking lawyer should have gotten me more, but I guess the guy was advertising during *Maury*. I thumbed through that bastard to see how many goddamn loops this coaster had, or how long the drop was. This thing better come with a damn Russian bride for $1.2 million. I found a page that included everything I needed to know about what everyone was calling 'Afterlife.'

The ride, which wasn't really a ride, was more just an enormous tower. Actually, the biggest tower ever, according to the brochure, which I bought because the damn thing disappeared into the clouds. The marketing team did a hell of a job on this:

We here at Six Flags Great America have always believed that carnival rides are the closest humankind would ever get to God. We've made that belief a reality. 'Afterlife' is quite literally a stairway to heaven. In our partnership with Monster Energy, we have spent the last decade working with philosophers, scientists, engineers, and priests, all in an effort to breach the walls of heaven and allow you to frolic in the clouds with loved ones who have passed. We had several leading experts ask God in prayer if he considered this an invasion of privacy—and perhaps divinity—but with a little convincing, they assured us God couldn't be happier about his new Six Flags Great America sponsorship. We even had his name trademarked and registered!

We have two package options listed below. The choice is yours. The afterlife is ready for you. Are you prepared for it?

1.   General Admission: Non-refundable, $500,000. General admission access allows the customer to make the climb up the stairs themselves. The climb itself takes between 30 and 40 years based on pace, but the view once you get up there is worth it!

2.   VIP Access: Non-refundable, $1.2 million. VIP access expedites the trip by giving you a personal rickshaw pulled by several Six Flags employees who have been

This was followed by hastily arranged stock photographs of clouds along with a picture of an old man waving from a hospital bed. All still had that iStock watermark on them, which I found sad because they had spent all of this money building the tallest thing to ever exist but couldn't shell out $1.50 to lift the watermark from some old man collecting royalties from the picture of him dying. I guess those royalties would go to the photographer anyways.

What the fuck? Someone flushing damn near half of their life to get a glimpse at their potential afterlife seemed like a classic carnie trap. I'll take my goldfish in a plastic bag that dies on the way home any day of the week. Hell, a Chinese finger trap is worth more than 40 years. But maybe that glimpse would give that person hope; maybe it would make it so they weren't living to die anymore. Maybe just knowing that their dead family was somewhere and not nowhere was enough to ease the pain that incapacitated them. Thinking about it like that made some sense. I was never religious, but I started thinking about my dad up there. For him, maybe nothing was better than anything. Without his memory, wouldn't the clouds just be even more miserable than staring at that damn TV? Would he even know the difference between the two? Wouldn't things just be more confusing? I guess it was possible that his dementia was fixed by God or whatever because God can do whatever he wants, I think? God, what I wouldn't give to talk to him and make sure things were alright. To know that he wasn't up there wandering around like a confused bastard without a clue in the world and not a single person to talk about roller coasters with or watch TV with him until he went to sleep. Maybe he slept more up there.

Well, I knew what I would give. I looked at the $1.2 million option. Only five years of my life. Five years to move on. I'd probably spent cumulatively five years in this park in my lifetime so far. Another five years flushed as someone having a heart attack in the stall next to me punched his ticket without having to spend a damn dime. I thought about my mom downstairs and how lonely she would be. She was old too. She probably wasn't going to die in five years, but if I were a betting man I'd say eight to ten years and she would be up there too. Wouldn't me being able to confirm if she was going to live in harmony for an eternity be worth it? Wouldn't it make her last two to three years with me more enjoyable? Wouldn't it make her not fear death like I did?

After seeing what happened to my dad, I was scared as fuck. Really messed me up good. I wondered if I should even tell her I was going. She wouldn't believe it anyway. Who would? A fucking amusement park promising to deliver you to the afterlife? Why was no one talking about this? This was probably the greatest discovery in the history of humanity, but it was just sitting in a peeling brochure. Glued between glossy pages by my thigh sweat and some grease that spilled onto my jeans after biting this hot dog a little too hard. I'd think about it, but there was a weird feeling that my mind was already made up.

Well, sure enough, that next morning, I woke up the earliest I ever had. I packed a suitcase and headed down to the bank. I didn't wake my mom up. I left a note saying that I was embarking on a business trip and wouldn't be back for a while but not to worry about me too much. I said when I came back, everything would be different, and I meant it. I hoped she understood. I didn't mean to be too cryptic, but there wasn't a lot else to say, I was about to give five years of my life to something I read about in a soiled marketing brochure. Five years inside an amusement park being hoisted like the loser I was into the clouds. Five years on what was described as a 'truly unforgettable romp.' I hoped it was more than that.

I didn't know how the hell bank withdrawals worked, but after talking with a manager for a while, I ended up extracting the entire $1.2 million. Even in hundreds, it was a hefty load. Heavy as hell. I had a hunter green duffle bag that I jammed it into and prayed I didn't get robbed on the way there. I bought the bag with the intent to, at some point, join a gym but never got around to it. I looked pretty slobbish, so I didn't think anyone would fuck with me at all, but it was always a risk. I made it to the park a few hours before it opened and sat in the empty parking lot, wondering if I was really going to do this. The heat rose from the asphalt and I followed the blurred lines and looked at the tarped structure. What a hulking fucking bastard it was. What did it look like under that tarp? Certainly, it wouldn't have the same elegance as, say, the perfect spinning circle of the Revolution or the undying nostalgia of the Batman ride, but knowing this amusement park . . . they had pulled out all the stops.

I saw an employee get out of their 2001 Prius and put out their cigarette on the hood, stuffing the half-smoked nub into the front pocket of his bacon-necked undershirt. At the same time, I got out of my car. He looked up as I closed my car door, wondering who the hell was at the park this early, and I waved like an absolute douche. Whatever. It's not like I was trying to impress this high school fuck anyways. He didn't know anything about the damn park; sure he worked there, but he was unmistakably miserable. Minimum wage wasn't enough to babysit a few thousand adults hell-bent on shitting their pants and demanding refunds.

He started walking and I walked too, both in a straight line toward the ticket sales kiosk. I was wearing this American flag shirt that I had gotten there on the 4th of July a dozen or so years ago; the thing was pitted out beyond belief and actually kind of smelled like shit. I hoped that one of the shirts I packed would be more presentable for when I entered heaven or talked to God or whatever. Not that my old man cared, we wore shitty clothes all the time.

I got to the kiosk just as the employee struggled with the keys to open the flimsy security door. I wondered why no one ever robbed that thing, but I guess it was because of the park's sanctity. I liked to think those entering the park had some elevated moral compass, but in all likelihood, it was because they were too goddamn stupid. I watched for a few minutes and he kept glancing up at me, his eyes pleading with me to just look at my phone or do something else, but for some reason, I kept staring. Finally, he opened it up and put on an old polo that hung from one of the coat hooks in the non-air-conditioned booth. He flicked this weird little oscillating fan on, and the Six Flags themed ribbons tied to it blew pathetically with the weak stream of the fan.

I didn't waste time with any small talk and said I wanted the VIP package for the 'Afterlife.' I hoisted the huge ass duffle bag up and pointed to it with this sheepish grin because I didn't know what else to do with my face. I put the $1.2 million on the counter and he dragged it across and we both listened to it hit the floor. He blandly thanked me for my purchase and collectedly slid the ticket across the counter. I wondered if that was it, so I asked if he needed to count the money and he replied with some smart ass answer like "Do I need to?" Fucking asshole. I don't know what I was expecting, maybe just wanting the transaction to appear even slightly more legitimate.

No receipt, no email, just a greasy ticket handed to me by some stoned high school flunk that would probably manage a Pier One Imports someday. This kid was gonna be stuck in Gurnee forever and I thought about telling him that, but he would have been indifferent regardless. He was still getting drunk and probably laid so the prospect of being stuck in this piece of shit city didn't seem all that bad with after-prom parties and such. Cut to five years down the road and that kid's fingers would be making toast in his bathtub, just praying that was the day the thing slipped in. As I was leaving, I asked the kid when Afterlife opened and he pointed at a sign that I should have noticed saying that it opened at 5 p.m. that same day. I asked if I could just go in now and he said if I wanted to get my ass kicked, I could, so I didn't.

I walked back to my car and felt a lot lighter without that huge fucking bag. I didn't really care much about the cash in all honesty, it wasn't really mine to begin with. My dad had suffered for it; I hadn't. I guess we suffered together. It wasn't his fault or anything and I was more than happy to do it. It was the least I could do, mainly I just wish he knew how much I cared. There were days where he would yell at me for not coming around, even though I was there damn near every day. Those days hurt the most. It wasn't the validation; it was that I didn't want him to feel alone. Nothing worse than eating warm tapioca alone. Slowly losing your mind is worse, but they're both consequences of each other in this case. I got back to my car and just sat there and stared. The parking lot filled up pretty quickly. No surprise there since it was the height of summer. The park was packed and I probably could have gone in and ridden some of the rides with my season pass, but for the first time in a long time, I didn't feel like it.

I barely even checked social media, because, as I mentioned, I hated it. I never posted and didn't really like a lot of stuff but just kind of suckled from its dying nipples. I mainly kind of just sat there in my hot ass car and listened to some radio station that was playing five hours of uninterrupted Zeppelin for some new promotion. The Zeppelin wasn't great—never really understood why people loved them so much, but it was something to fill the silence. Sometimes that's all you really need. Before I knew it, the clock hit 5 p.m. and the park started clearing out. I got out of my car and started walking back toward the majestic stucco ticketing booth. I was really sweaty and felt kind of sick, but I always felt a little ill. That was the best I could ask for.

The ticket itself was damn sleek looking. Sleek and wet. Matte black with braille lettering that said 'Afterlife' on it. I rubbed my fingers against the bumps and got some brutal chills. I saw a magnificently bright light materializing in the distance and it all felt weirdly foreboding. Five fucking years. A substantial collection of bile gathered in my throat before my tongue worked it back down. Not today. I approached the ticketing guy again and he didn't recognize me even though I had just given him over a million dollars in cash a few hours prior. He probably had me confused for someone who handed over a similarly feeling duffle bag full of human hair earlier that day. I slid the ticket over the counter and wondered what kind of VIP check they did. Like I said, I didn't care about the money, but a million better buy some customer service!

He pulled out this hole puncher that was shaped like a naked lady and gave the ticket a punch. It didn't go through the first time, so he worked it over pretty good. The thing was bent to hell by the time he gave it back, but at least it had a silhouette of a nude woman on it now, which I guess meant that I could get access to heaven. Any thoughts of framing that ticket were out the window after that kid mangled it. I had kept every season pass I ever bought in this box under my bed, but I don't think this thing was going to make the cut.

I walked through the empty park and kind of fantasized about just riding Goliath all night. That was Dad's favorite roller coaster. Thing was bumpy as hell, but he was a sucker for the old wood, said those wooden beams told stories the steel ones couldn't. He said we deposited memories into cracks in the wood and when the wheels ran over them, the memories were released. That's why every ride was so different. The rides didn't seem all that much different to me, but maybe I just wasn't paying attention. I had bigger things to do than to hear stories from some crumbling beast. That million dollars created a bridge between Gurnee and heaven that I was meant to cross.

That's what the brochure told me.

Afterlife was at the end of the park, but that heaving bastard was impossible to take my eyes off the moment I left my car. The tarp was off and from a distance, it looked like a completely smooth steel structure without much adornment. Who needs a sign written in Comic Sans with a bunch of idiotic farm creatures telling you what height you need to be to ride when it was something this momentous? As I got closer, I noticed that it wasn't all that smooth. In fact, the Monster Energy logo had been carved like heliographs on every inch of the thing. Jesus, who had the time to do that? It was as elegant a partnership as any and it did give it a really mystical feel, but I can't imagine the time to carve that thing up. It did its job because whenever I thought about heaven the rest of my life, I would also think about carbonated water, sucrose, glucose, citric acid, natural flavors, taurine, sodium citrate, color added, panax ginseng root extract, L-carnitine, L-tartrate, caffeine, sorbic acid, benzoic acid, niacinamide, sodium chloride, Glycine max glucuronolactone, inositol, and guarana seed extract, in no particular order. I wondered if they gave God a few flat-brimmed hats for the effort, and if they hadn't, you bet your ass a flood was coming or some people would be turned to salt or something.

After another 10 minutes of walking or so, I saw what looked like the entrance to the ride and I approached it purposefully. If I was going to waste five years mounting this thing, I wanted it to start as soon as possible. More foreplay than any man had ever experienced, but this time instead of spunking into a sock, I'd get salvation. Temporary salvation as it were, there were no guarantees, but I didn't really care. I just wanted to make sure my dad was okay. The entrance itself was unmanned and I wondered who the hell was going to take my ticket. I walked around the thing seven or eight times before noticing a tiny slit in its side, so I took out that mangled ticket and fed it into the slit. It seemed to go through alright, but not with the same mechanical affirmation as a vending machine. The thing was more like a mail slot than anything. I peeked inside of it and saw an employee sitting on the other side, who was making a buzzing noise and sliding the ticket slowly in. A portion of the base of the structure slid open and I entered.

The employee told me he was sorry about the ticketing machine. It sometimes malfunctioned. I didn't have the heart to tell him that I knew it was him in there and no ticketing machine at all. I doubt he would have cared much, but he seemed devoted to the illusion of it all. The door slid shut behind me and I asked the kid where all the other customers were. He replied that I was the only one. I turned around to some noise outside of the structure and saw a pretty hefty line forming through that slot, but the employee shut the slot immediately and repeated that I was the only one and shook his head as though he was disgraced that I didn't believe him. I didn't mean to bring shame to the sorry bastard, but he gave me a look like I killed his family. I explained to him that it was just curiosity, but he wasn't having it.

He grabbed my arm and dragged me through the enormous lobby that had at least 20 gift shops and an Auntie Anne's like you wouldn't believe. I was suddenly pretty hungry, but the kid didn't seem to have any interest in stopping. We also passed a tiny church that looked to be created for a religion that wasn't invented yet. I'm not sure how I even knew it was a church, but I would worship at anything sandwiched between a Sunglass Hut and an Auntie Anne's. I actually saw a priest almost choke on an Auntie Anne's pretzel nugget one time while I was working there. I gave him the Heimlich maneuver and the chunk flew out of his mouth and splattered on the neon menu behind me. The chewed pretzel bits and apparent clam chowder breakfast kind of looked like Virgin Mary as they slid down the board. It was the closest I've ever been to a miracle, but after it was all done, the priest condemned me to hell and demanded a 15 percent off coupon for the rest of his life.

My manager obliged and agreed that I would spend an eternity suffering for undercooking those pretzel nuggets. The priest came by once a week to remind me I was an unredeemable piece of shit that deserved to die like a dog and get his discounted lemonade. I thought it was a little harsh, but I'd do my time if I had to. I guess neither one of them could see the beauty in it all. Isn't a near-death experience worth it for some lemonade? I figured it would make some good homily fodder or, at the very least, rejuvenate the withering Catholic church, but it ended up being a discreet condemnation with no publicity at all. Only three people knew the fate of my soul and one of those had his wife fucked by the manager at Wahlburgers. I wished that the priest would have just chewed.

Anyways, we walked until we reached a row of rickshaws or chariots or whatever you want to call them. These things were solid gold! Unbelievable craftsmanship, really! I asked the kid where they were made, and he didn't reply. They looked pretty unwieldy though. I happened to glance at the side of one of the carriages, and it looked like they were imported from South Bend, Indiana. Damnit, they had me fooled. I guess these things were just pieces of shit ornaments you glued on top of the recreational vehicle that was going to bankrupt you and prevent your kid from going to college.

I bet that RV looked pretty sweet, though. No one really considers the correlation between recreational vehicles and the Roman Empire, but I think some of that gluttony is fortified in our blood. So, in a sense, one wouldn't exist without the other. Buying a traveling house outside of our means that we, in turn, neglect in favor of dying in our favorite easy chair is equivalent to Caesar conquering France. We always want what we can't have, as the saying goes, even though we can have anything nowadays. Most of that shit just causes crippling debt and more monotony, but at least we have the option to keep buying. It was an elevated monotony and the corners of the boxes provided peaks and valleys in an otherwise wholly smooth existence. That was freedom. Freedom to plummet into oblivion and be replaced by an empire of shit—at least you were doing something. The perpetual state of acquisition was a place everyone loved to exist. Smoke from our burning bank accounts created the steam that propelled us through another god-awful day.

I enjoyed shoveling more cash into the furnace as much as the next guy. It was better than whatever alternative there was. I guess we all had to buy ointment to heal the cuts from our routine daily floggings. That ointment would never actually heal anything, but if you smeared enough on, I guess it would seem like the cuts weren't there at all.

Sometimes I think the act of buying is the closest my

generation will get to battle. I'm not sure what beheading a man feels like, but I once spent $300 on sunglasses and regretted it for the next decade. I bet the adrenaline experienced from an online checkout was the same as dodging hot oil dumped from castle walls. Those things would taunt me day and night from their place on my bookshelf—too expensive to enjoy, they sat there and flaunted their inactivity while I barely made that month's rent. If RVs were available when Caesar was alive, he probably wouldn't have been betrayed—everyone wants to know someone who owns an RV without ever owning one themselves. Think about him holding a flaming sword out of that bastard, leading his fearless troops into battle behind the casual luxury of a brand new Coachmen. Add a deep fryer and a few flat screens in that thing and you'd put a brothel out of business.

Anyways, I was shocked to see that each one of these golden chariots was fastened to an employee wearing a Six Flags branded polo shirt and a pair of ill-fitting cargo shorts and Skechers Shape-Ups. The host sat me down in one of the first rows of chariots and I could see the night sky. We were outside again, but a few levels up. I wasn't quite sure how this thing was going to work, but it looked like an enormous ramp spiraled all the way up the tower like a goddamn vein or artery.

Was this employee to pull me the entire way up for five whole years? I tapped him on the shoulder and he looked back fearfully. His eyes had blinders on either side to keep him focused on the task at hand. The host who let me in handed me half of a thick carrot and motioned to feed the employee harnessed to my chariot. I did just that, gently feeding him the carrot and feeling the hot breath from his nostrils on my hand. I wasn't quite sure how I felt about all of this, but I assumed the kid was making a decent wage if he was meant to pull me for five years, then again, something told me that wasn't the case. We kind of just sat there for a minute in excruciating silence, but I didn't really have anything to say and didn't feel like he deserved a tip, so I waited it out. I could endure most unbearable situations with the best of them. I would have made a hell of a soldier in World War I because I thrived in the trenches of life. Give me a shovel and I'd dig myself as deep as I needed to, sit in the muck and unceremoniously bleed out. They say time is money, well, I didn't have a lot of money but did have all the time in the world.

Finally, the little puissant realized he wasn't getting a buck from my folded arms and patted the other employee on the ass, apparently signifying that he demanded motion. The hierarchy between the two was bizarre and I wondered what qualifications made one an esteemed host and the other a glorified donkey. As far as I could tell, the two were interchangeable. I didn't think about it too long because sometimes that's just how life goes. I've pulled my fair share of paying customers up to their shit mountains for some senseless cause or desire that neither of us understood. I'd also stood around patting asses.

The wheels of the chariot began to turn as his legs drove into the cobblestone ramp. Shaky at first, they steadied themselves and picked up steam, gaining a hypnotizing rhythm. Even though I was the first customer, it seemed like they had already made this journey thousands of times. Before I knew it, I was flying in the night air up the ramp to heaven. I couldn't believe the kid could pull this fast, his wiry frame suggesting otherwise, but the dedication to the company trumped any physical shortcomings. At any given point, I could see most of his skeleton through his translucent skin in the moonlight, his heart beating harder and harder as he pulled a complete and total stranger toward God.

Blood flowed freely from the piercings that fastened the cart to his skin, digging deeper with every lurch forward. I didn't know what he had to prove to anyone—maybe they were paid based on mileage per day. I yelled at the kid that he was doing a hell of a job, but he didn't turn around. I wasn't sure if I could sit in this thing for five years without talking, but at this pace, we'd be there by morning and the silence was doing me some good.

Level by level, we climbed. Every now and again, we would pass shops that were carved into the middle of the structure, selling carnival food and self-proclaimed rare merchandise.

A cherry Coke sounded pretty damn good right about now, so did a special edition bobblehead, but goddamn, this kid had a rhythm going and I didn't feel like interrupting him.

Instead, I sat quietly and wrestled with the desire for carbonated syrup while a kid making minimum wage sacrificed his body for my cause. I felt like a real piece of shit and even screamed it out a few times jokingly and hoped the kid could hear it. I thought the recognition of how fucked up this all was would somehow make both of us feel better. The key to everything was designating yourself as a piece of shit first and foremost, thus excusing anything that was said or done after. All anyone really wants is the recognition that you are a mere accumulation of filth in their respective boot tread, and your sole purpose in life is to be eventually scraped from those grooves with a fallen tree branch. I was just fine occupying whatever tread I could, a companion that you could step on and maybe unknowingly carry with you for a bit before getting frustrated enough to wipe me on a curb or square of raised sidewalk.

I doubted he could hear me though, the wheels grinding and screaming with every turn. The constant twists were making me dizzy and I eventually vomited from the side of the chariot. It was unfortunate timing just as the boy was making a turn and the chariot tipped, hurtling me on the smooth concrete. I'd never been in an actual accident before, which was surprising given the amount of drunk driving I did in high school. I guess it was like they said: time slowed down and I kind of just felt like I did when I died in my dreams. I'd almost died approximately 3,000 times in lucid dreams throughout my life, mostly in plane crashes, though I once pissed the bed after a masked intruder stabbed me in the liver. The key to waking up during these was actually dying. The rest of the trauma could be mimicked completely by your sleeping brain, but when it came time to actually die, the thing would bail like a pussy, and you'd be left in your bed soaking wet and crying.

It was almost morning at this point as sunlight beams groped tentatively over plywood walls of the otherwise stone structure. And before checking on the employee, I snuck a glance over the side of the ramp. I couldn't believe how close to the ground we still were. I could still distinguish faces in the line below me, each one more horrific than the next. I wondered if my face looked as perverse and gnarled to the employees and assumed it probably did. They looked back at me with the same hatred and disgust. I guess anyone that went to the park hated themselves a little and hated the others that also went even more than that. Amusement parks were built for the depressed and the forgotten. The sounds of grating steel, bubbling oil from unloved deep fryers, and insufferable screaming drew them like moths to a flame.

I went over to check on the employee who had collapsed with the chariot, but he was already being dragged away by a few other employees from a nearby Johnny Rockets. I asked what they were doing and one of them just shrugged. He handed me a half-eaten burger as though it were some sort of consolation. As though a soggy burger with visible strands of another person's saliva was an appropriate trade for a human life. It was the type of heartless transaction you'd expect from Universal Studios Orlando, but not here. I asked another employee and another after him before finally demanding to talk to their manager. Shortly thereafter, a pear-shaped man wearing a short-sleeved button-up shirt with a clip-on bow tie and a pair of bootcut khaki pants approached me with his hands folded onto his sagging belly.

"How can I help you today, good sir?" asked the portly man, the name tag indicating his name was Phillip.

He looked like someone who wanted respect but never got it, someone whose perception of themselves was totally fucked out. He reminded me of my manager at Auntie Anne's and every other manager that seemed to manifest out of nowhere in strip malls across the country. These types of sorry bastards skipped birth and adolescence and were sentenced immediately to middle management in some franchise that would go under in two to three years. The weird thing was, they seemed to revel in the opportunity at such a plain existence. Maybe because their lifelong purpose of buying and selling mid-end clothing or managing the quality of reheated frozen food was so apparent. Having a decided fate, no matter how miserable, at least meant you were still destined for something.

"What happened to the person pulling my chariot?" I asked the man, trying to catch a glimpse of where the lifeless corpse was being dragged.

"He's in a better place now," he said calmly. "You look like you could use a cherry Coke."

I could use a cherry Coke, but how did this beady-eyed little fuck know that? He produced just that from his trouser pocket and the idiotic looking yardstick glass was ungodly cold. I didn't trust the man or the temperature of the bottle, but I drank. I drank because I was thirsty and drank to mourn the presumed death of the employee. I drank to buy time, because I didn't know what else to say to the man who stood there with a shit-eating grin and an uncomfortable desire to please. I studied him for a minute and wondered how he had gotten up here, if he and his employees lived in the confines of their shitty restaurant. He adjusted his pants, which were somehow falling down despite his paunchy frame and scratched his head, sending visible dandruff flakes into the stale breeze.

One of the restaurant waiters crudely stripped the body naked and put on the polo shirt and cargo shorts that my steed was wearing. He walked nonchalantly up to the chariot, tipped it upright, and applied the harnesses to himself. There he stood, motionless. Waiting for me to pile back in and be on my way. I wasn't done yet though. Neither was the manager apparently, who walked up to the kid and inspected the hell out of him. Top to bottom and back up top again, he even pulled out a ruler and measured the length of the kid's shorts before finally telling him he would be docking his pay for not having a uniform that adhered to their corporate standards.

I felt pretty bad damn bad for him, given that it seemed like he didn't have a hell of a lot of say in what size his hand-me-downs were, but I wasn't going to say anything. You would think the clothing policy would be a little more lenient given that they were stripping them from a dead person, but not here, and who was I to say what was right or what was wrong? It was possible he wasn't dead too, but in my limited experience with dead bodies, he seemed pretty goddamn dead. The other employee dragged the nude body through the doors at Johnny Rockets. For the brief moment the doors opened, I felt an excruciating cold from the overworked AC unit and heard *Yakety Yak* by the Coasters playing faintly on the replica jukebox.

"Is that other boy dead?" I asked, already knowing the answer to the question.

"Yes, though you shouldn't be too upset; his family is awarded free general admission tickets to this very ride because of his sacrifice," replied the manager calmly.

His tone suggested that he thought this death was some FastPass to sainthood—or that it was somehow equivalent to the crucifixion of Christ in terms of its importance to humanity. Had he died for my sins?

"Wouldn't his family prefer to spend time with him while he's alive?" I asked.

"Some do, some don't," he replied, his grin never shifting. His eyes stared directly through mine and into the cloudless sky behind me.

The exchange went on for several more minutes, each answer escalating in depravity. The body would be ground into burger patties to fuel the next wave of people trying to see dead family. He described it as the circle of life, but the parallel seemed like a stretch. I knew Johnny Rockets to be a fast-casual chain restaurant with a poorly researched 1950s cultural facade, but I never knew they also promoted cannibalism. Maybe it was buried in some 10,000-page franchise manifesto, or maybe that's why meat was so cheap back in the '50s. Either way, what did I know? Maybe we were all just eating each other until we died. I guess being collapsed into a patty melt is better than lying in a plywood box forever. Maybe I'd be the grease that eventually clogged someone's artery enough to have them dying in an amusement park bathroom. That was best-case scenario.

He said the boy died doing what he loved, but I didn't believe that either. Was mindlessly pulling someone to their deceased relatives something anyone loved? I explained to him that I wanted no part in this and he told me it was too late. He seemed pretty apologetic about the whole thing, but I could tell deep down he found the entire thing hilarious. At points, he appeared to be choking down laughter, though it was possible it was reflux. Reflux is always a possibility. If I didn't get back into the chariot, the next employee would be executed for not fulfilling his duty as a Six Flags employee. And if he died that way, his family would receive nothing.

I started crying, but the logic made sense. Six Flags was known for airtight contracts and this was no different. The manager offered me a handful of flag-shaped Mardi Gras beads to cheer me up, but they didn't. I put them around my neck anyway. At least I understood the stakes now. I wondered if I could keep this next one living for more than a day. Did they want to live?

After a while, the manager looked at his watch and said I better be on my way. He applied the blinders to the employee and helped me into the chariot as though I was geriatric, holding my forearm and gently guiding me into the overstuffed cushions. I sat there like a spineless loser because what else could I do? I wasn't going to deprive this next employee's family of a few general admission tickets to visit his spirit or whatever in the clouds. That would be fucked up. Well, I gave that goddamn manager a nod and he patted the employee's ass to make him go. The wheels started turning again and we were on our way. I looked back and the guy was waving like a complete moron and I kind of wanted to kill him for how idiotic it looked.

Sun down. Sun up. Sun down. Sun up.

Days passed without much notice or fanfare. This guy was really a beast. It had been a full week and he hadn't eaten or drunken a drop and neither had I. The manager had given me an additional cherry Coke, which I was rationing;

and it sure helped with the pissing and shitting, which I was doing very little of. I didn't know what would happen if I asked the lunatic pulling this thing to stop. I figured he would likely die, but maybe it was just my Irish Catholic Guilt that had me agonizing in silence. His suffering was worse than mine, but he somehow seemed happier. I had also paid over a million dollars and up to this point was complicit in a murder and was regularly pissing and shitting from a golden chariot made for a recreational vehicle. I didn't want to kill this guy, but could I really be miserable for five full years? After much debate, I yelled at the employee to stop when we had made it to the next Johnny Rockets, which had a gift shop adjacent to it.

The employee stopped and predictably collapsed similarly to the other one. Several employees exited the restaurant in a single file line along with a manager named Hank and before he could ask me how he could be of assistance, I told him to get me the Jailhouse Rock human burger and a fucking cherry Coke. He nodded happily, delighted that the process didn't require any further explanation. They dragged that body in even faster than the last time and I could still hear *Yakety Yak* playing. Years later, I would vomit on command to that song and when my therapist would ask me why, I would just say I fucking hated the '50s. It was a bullshit era anyways.

They had the next beast of burden lined up in an instant, and after my meal I felt slightly recharged. I told the manager to make sure that kid's family got his tickets and he assured me they would because it was company policy. No one ever disobeyed company policy. I believed him. I didn't have any reason not to. I went into the gift shop and purchased a snow globe that had Jesus on the Crucifix in the middle and was filled with Monster Energy. When you shook it, tiny American flags swirled around his new naked body. I wondered if God had signed off on this as it seemed sacrilegious, but then again, any press is good press.

I was helped back into my chariot and off we went. The first year was pretty goddamn awful, or at least what I thought was the first year. My stomach was in shambles from all the human. I hadn't had a solid bowel movement in months and when I asked for water, they would just keep giving me cherry Coke. My collection of rare souvenirs continued to grow and was getting pretty impressive, though. The chariot became more oppressive with every tchotchke and knick-knack, but I figured they wouldn't have put the stores there if they didn't expect me to keep buying. Plus, every time one of these employees died, it seemed like the next one was faster and more eager to finish the job. The thought of my souvenir pile pulverizing the insides of these poor chariot tuggers was sickening, but I blamed the nausea and overall unwell feeling on the lousy meat and Cokes at a certain point. Later I'd justify any purchase as a means to shorten their suffering. My unchecked consumerism was doing them a favor in hurtling them faster toward the inevitable.

I had even asked a few shop managers about the employees' happiness and he told me that they had nothing else to do anyway. We were fairly similar in that way.

The regularity of it all became comical. I was fucking numb by the third year in. I knew it was the third year because I ended up asking one of the managers what the date was and he pointed to this giant sculpture of a frog wearing an idiotic backwards hat and a denim coat that was repeating the date, time, and temperature in all different languages. I ate my burgers and drank my Coke and piss and shit like hell. Sometimes I even got impatient when they switched uniforms. I wondered why everyone couldn't just wear the same uniform, but a manager told me it would then be impossible to designate who worked where. It seemed like anyone on this tower worked in some capacity for the tower, but I guess all businesses approach inconsequential uniforms differently. My manager at Auntie Anne's threatened me with a knife out by his car because I wasn't wearing the right visor for my Wednesday shift, but I knew he didn't have the stones to stab me, so I worked the whole thing in my Monday visor. That would end up being the most rebellious thing I did in my life, at least from what I can remember—accidentally wearing a brown visor instead of a yellow one. No wonder his wife was unsatisfied.

At some point, I ended up masturbating to a cardboard cutout in a store window that reminded me of this crush I had junior year in high school on a girl named Claire Bowman. She wasn't all that cute and neither was the cutout, but sometimes you gotta do what you gotta do. I told the manager to turn around while my new Six Flags sweatpants hit the pavement, but I was sure he didn't. I could feel his eyes on me as I climaxed onto the store window. I left the mess for him to clean up and told him I hoped he enjoyed the show.

I threatened to kill one of the managers once when my burger came out too well-done, but other than that, I was pretty indifferent. I actually made the manager dig it out of the fly-ridden trash heap and eat it himself, the guy smiling the whole time as he choked down that hockey puck. I just thought the dead employee deserved better than to be cooked well-done. A couple of other waiters giggled behind the manager as he was choking it down, so I winked at them like it was the coolest thing to ever happen. In hindsight, the manager was still eating one of their own, but man did he look miserable. Laughing at misery is pretty natural.

I'd sleep sometimes, but it wasn't restful. I could always feel the turns, even when we stopped and I bought new souvenirs I could feel those turns in my knees. I wondered if I'd ever walk right again and knew I probably wouldn't. I would look at my phone from time to time and wonder what was happening outside of the ride. It died a long time ago and oddly enough, the stores sold shrimp deveiners that looked like the old dancing guy from their commercials but didn't sell phone chargers. I didn't miss it too much, but there was a feeling of dwindling sanity without the blue light to anchor me to the judgment and resentment I cherished. Sometimes reality is as simple as just the ability to tear other people down. Without the losers from my hometown continually reminding me that things could be a lot worse, I realized I wasn't all that happy myself. I probably knew that all along. Though, I guess it's pretty damn easy to get caught staring at a racist on acid trying to butt fuck a chicken or get caught in a multi-level marketing scheme while drifting aimlessly toward nothing in particular.

Sooner or later, I'd have to put my eyes back on the road. Maybe this trip was the gas station sex pill I needed to prevent me from nodding off behind the wheel. Maybe I'd finally stop worshipping the demise of others in favor of my own happiness. I made myself a nice empty promise to change when I got back; it contained no weight whatsoever and disappeared with my piss blowing from the back of the chariot, but at least I made it. I was objectively happier without that goddamn device, but I wasn't sure I was ready to exchange happiness for madness. I would probably always climb their ladder of shit to clean my own gutters.

At the next Johnny Rockets, I asked the manager if I could go in and wash up. I hadn't bathed in the three-plus years I was on this trip and imagined I smelled like a couple of hounds going at it in the turned egg salad from a Memorial Day cookout ten years ago. The manager argued that it was pretty unorthodox, but as I got closer, he agreed. My stench apparently pummeled him into compliance. The customer was always right, especially when he smelled like I did.

I knew it was going to be bad judging from the new clothes I had to keep buying at the gift shops. It seemed like at every gift shop I was sizing up in another commemorative sweat suit. Not to mention the deaths of employees pulling my chariot seemed to be really piling up. I lost count after 100 and would probably just tell anyone who asked it was, in fact, only 100. That would be an acceptable number for most.

Each one pulled for less time than the last. They didn't complain though. None of them said a word. I guess they couldn't wait for their parents to visit them like I was visiting mine.

Anyways, I didn't even check the tags anymore on those sweats, I just let the poor tailor measure the size of my taint and grabbed a new size from the rack. Looking back, I wondered why they needed a tailor at all—I guess it was to make the VIPs feel special. It was actually a cruel ritual in humiliation for both myself and the employee. Me, not wanting the man to witness my disgusting naked body and him forced to hold a measuring tape to the jungle of matted pubic hair between my shaft and asshole while lifting fold after fold of lard. It was a peculiar method of measurement, but I was done asking questions at this point. I tried to make small talk and asked the different tailors about the Chicago Bears or if mercury was in retrograde, but they never responded.

One of the men mentioned something about missing his wife, but it was drowned by the sound of the cash register and the bagging of a new sweat suit. I didn't ask what he said, but I told him to keep the change, thinking the extra 13 cents would heal him. Whenever I was feeling bad about myself, which I often did given my seemingly grotesque physical nature, I thought about that 13 cents. It wasn't a lot, but sometimes it made me feel alright.

I ended up throwing most of the sweat suits away years later, not because I had lost the weight, but because the shit stains had bled all the way through and were visible to the world. I was fine with them when they were my little secret with my pair of pants, but it takes a real sicko to share that kind of neglect with the world. Stagnation is incredible until it's not. Sitting in your own shit is fine until it breaches a certain threshold, that threshold being a pair of polyester blend sweatpants. Polyester blend anything was the way most people measured the depth of their uncaring.

I entered the bathroom at Johnny Rockets and it was pretty

damn spotless. There was a trough of potpourri in the corner that I nibbled a few twigs from because my breath smelled like a damn petting zoo and it was something besides reheated humans or cherry Coke. The smell reminded me of my grandma's house and all of a sudden, I really wished I'd never done any of this. I wished I'd never gotten the million dollars, wished I hadn't been holding my dad's hand when he died, and wished that I wasn't going to meet God in my current state. As we climbed higher, I seemed to get more detestable.

Sometimes I was aware of the transition, other times not. Sometimes I just stared into the sun while I deteriorated.

I looked at myself in the mirror and it was about what I expected, certainly unfit for heaven but still passable by fairground standards. My eyes sunk all the way to the back of my head. My hair was so brittle that I broke a piece off like a handful of uncooked spaghetti and dropped it into the sink. My lips looked like used bandages. Painful goiters and tags jutted from my face and neck, which connected to my chin, making it indeterminable from my swollen head. Each one looked eager to detonate cherry Coke pus all over the checkerboard tile of the bathroom. My tongue looked like a hairbrush; the white film that covered it increased its girth by at least a few centimeters. My muscles atrophied with my transcendent inactivity and my skin sagged in a seeming effort to retreat from my disfigured face. It longed for the earth below and an escape from this tower.

I ran the faucet, and cherry Coke drained from the goddamn spout. I cupped some in my hand and splashed it on my face anyways. I took another handful and drizzled it on the top of my head and imagined myself being baptized by that priest who condemned me to hell. The high fructose corn syrup dripping slowly over my forehead and filling all of my enormous pores was more refreshing than you'd think. The '50s themed bathroom had made me pure once more, forgiven by the holy soda that spewed from the Marilyn Monroe shaped faucet.

Although I doubted there was any written physical requirement for heaven, there was probably some assumption that someone whose sausage skin could barely stretch over their yogurt insides would fall right through those clouds. I thought about the angels and their wings and how pathetic they would look trying to lift me. Actually, the whole scene made me laugh pretty hard. I hadn't had a laugh in ages. Maybe that bathroom did do me some good. I was feeling like a god myself after my bathroom baptism, so I ordered another burger well-done but then acted confused when it got there. Man, I ripped that manager a new one—I mean, really went deep with my insults. I called him a coward incapable of love and said his wife was probably hundreds of miles down, getting her brains fucked out by a GameStop employee.

I grabbed him by the shirt and pulled him close, then stuffed the entire burger into his mouth and firmly clutched the top of his head and bottom of his chin with my giant hands. I started forcing his chubby face to chew like it never had before. My hands were really disrupting this bastard's natural chewing motion and the speed and force at which I jammed his face together was getting downright brutal. The frenzy at which my hands moved seemed to grow with the pain in his pathetic eyes.

I heard teeth chipping and joining the skin and a blood casserole that was partially spilling from his mouth. I poured a Coke on his head and bludgeoned him to death with a Six Flags ashtray. He was already choking on the burger and probably would have died without me caving his skull like wet cardboard, but there was no pageantry in choking to death. I looked at this as a favor, much like I did my souvenir purchasing. Let the good times roll. I winked at the employees behind him who weren't really laughing this time and told them they were free to return to earth or whatever, but they just kind of stood there. After a while, I decided to get moving. My work here was done. As the chariot pulled farther up the next ramp, I looked back, and the employees seemed to be dragging him back into the restaurant.

The circle of life, I thought.

After the chariot was moving again with a full head of steam, I reframed everything in my favor. I looked at my physical and spiritual downfall as a revolution. It was my own personal war against senseless vanity and relentless self-promotion. I had nothing to promote. I had no pride. Even if my phone worked, there was nothing to post. I was a messiah for those with no likes, for those with nothing to share. Those without likes shall inherit the earth, as the biblical saying goes.

The farther I climbed, the more liberated I became from it all. Maybe God wanted to break me down into nothing so that I could become something, or maybe we had all gotten too far away from being nothing. Maybe these were all just the thoughts of a raving lunatic who was being routinely poisoned with spoiled meat and different flavors of

Monster Energy. Oh yeah, I forgot to mention, once we birthed into the fourth layer of clouds, I was afforded Monster instead of cherry Coke, which was a welcomed change. The energy drink sent lightning bolts through the veins of my cock and made sleep optional. It gave me life when I felt like I had none. A feeling that doesn't come from a higher power, but rather from a neon green can manufactured in Mexico.

I always felt closer to God when I drank it, so maybe they were one and the same. Who knows or cares? Enlightenment comes when you least expect it. It's not the curated bullshit you see at Joshua Tree or Tulum, and it's not about chakras being cleansed or astrology. It's about drinking enough energy drinks to flatline without even knowing it and then taking an enormous shit from a moving RV ornament. It's about regressing into nothing.

I would routinely pull teeth from my gums like candles from a birthday cake, the sensation tickling me and I would laugh and try to get the attention of the person pulling the rickshaw, but they never turned around. I bet they would have found it funny if they had turned. I kept the teeth in this flag-shaped coin purse and thought about making a necklace out of them when I got home. Mom would get a kick out of that, I bet. I could give it to her for Mother's Day and say I got it on Etsy. She really liked Etsy.

I was pretty goddamn used to death at this point. I'd seen several hundred people die in front of me and another 10 or 12 managers I had slaughtered to satisfy an increasing bloodlust. I rationalized these butcherings using the perceived freedom I projected on the waiters. Who knows if they were actually free, though? Was anyone besides me on my quest for self-destruction actually free? Most of them simply went back into the restaurant, apparently uninterested in my revolution. Even with all of the physical death, I still wondered what it would be like to see the spirit of a dead person. I guess there was the consideration that all of those who died wouldn't even be in heaven. I wouldn't recognize any of them anyways.

Days continued to pass, and one morning I woke up with vomit spewing from my nostrils, which wasn't unusual. I sat up and brushed it off like I always did. No harm, no foul. I yawned and felt the cold air piercing the holes in my gums from all of my lost teeth—no better way to wake up. I'd later pitch the concept to Starbucks and be arrested shortly after that. I rubbed the cake batter from my eyes and let the crust fall onto my sweat suit, my eyes slowly adjusting to the light. Jesus Christ! Up ahead seemed to be the top of the goddamn tower! I could see an enormous ring in the clouds above the top that had this beautiful golden glow and I started to cry. The tears were sucked immediately into my dry skin. They barely made it halfway down my cheeks before being greedily consumed.

You'd think all the grease would hydrate, but it did quite the opposite. It felt like my skin was chewing the tears as they painfully reentered my face. I tried to stop crying to stop the miserable sensation, but it was all too beautiful.

I rocked from side to side in an attempt to pry my enormous body from the grips of the chariot, which held my skin sack like a goddamn vice. The sides of it had been digging into me for months, but I could barely feel it under all of the fat. Now that I'd moved, I felt the blisters pop and the blood pooled in my sweat-logged suit. Goddamn, those blisters must have been hulking! Rarely is there an audible pop when a blister ruptures. Even the employee pulling the cart seemed to want to turn around to see what the commotion was, but he didn't.

I couldn't see the hemorrhaging wounds over my rolling mounds, but they were painful bastards and ripe as hell. I could smell the rot and infection even over the vomit that plastered my nose hairs. I couldn't even remember the last time I had stopped. Time seemed to melt like the thin layer of skin holding the pus in on those blisters. I considered the analogy and thought it was poetic because time is pretty fragile. Now the floodgates were open, saturating my legs with hours, weeks, months, pus, blood, and serum. I thought I was awake the whole time because of the Monster, but then again, I wasn't the best judge of consciousness.

Five years already.

I decided to stop moving and just wait to reach the top. The biggest climax ever. Hopefully, the employees up there had some lube and could get enough leverage to wrestle me from this godforsaken prison. I could use another Monster Energy too. I wanted to be alert when I finally reached salvation.

"Faster!" I yelled at my steed. "Faster goddammit!"

The anticipation was killing me, so I began sorting through my souvenir pile to make the employee-run faster. Finally, I found a reaching device with a T-Rex head fastened to the end of it. The poorly made device was utterly incapable of actually picking anything up, but it would be perfect for motivating this sorry bastard. I raised the device and attempted to flog the back of the employee, but the swift motion caused my bicep to explode instantly. My muscles were only capable of sitting, and I was foolish to believe otherwise. The device dropped and rolled down the ramp. I'd demand we stop to pick it up on the way back.

I sat there like a helpless insect but decided good things came to those who waited. I had waited five years for this moment. What was another hour? I started fantasizing about the welcome ceremony when my chariot arrived. I would be the first living person to ever experience the afterlife. I imagined a row of cherubs playing golden trumpets, a red carpet, maybe even some water. I could use some water. What did upper management at Six Flags have in store for this king? I wondered if employees would throw themselves on my walking path like palms for Jesus on his donkey. We weren't all that different - me and Jesus, that is. I couldn't really think of any similarities in the moment, but there was something about betrayal or temptation or revenge. I finally landed on us both caring about our dads.

The employee was slowing down as we reached a completely level platform at the top of the enormous structure. He crossed onto the platform and collapsed, one final death. Maybe his family would get VIP tickets instead of general admission. I looked above the platform and saw a circular parting of clouds. I half expected the body to float directly up there, but instead, an employee driving a brand new Ford F-150 with a plow attachment drove across the flattened platform and pushed the corpse over the side. All the best, I didn't need some welcome ceremony for the kid ruining my moment, something that

I had worked so damn hard for. I saw a crowd gathering in the clouds, which was about 50 yards from where I sat in my chariot on the smooth marble veneer that seemed to rest loosely on top of a stucco base.

Old and young, all different walks of life, they all had wings and halos. I was a little disappointed by this because I thought it was pretty cliche, but I gave it a pass because what else was I going to do? I'd tell the Lord that I would appreciate a little more nuance when I finally made it up there. I was amazed that there were so many people up there. I figured about 90 percent of the world's souls were totally unsalvageable, but it looked like a free-for-all from what I could tell. Maybe we had all gotten so intolerable that the qualifications to get in were equally abysmal. Some of the saved looked pretty damn undeserving and kind of reminded me of the people I saw waiting behind me five years ago. Others looked really fucking happy too. I guess there was a pretty even balance between fiendish perverts and happy people who died in their sleep.

They all peered onto the platform gently from their cloud kingdom and it all looked pretty fucking magical. So I put my hands on either armrest of the chariot and tried to stand, but my skin had grown one with the throne. I would later find out that some pieces of skin had even started to grow around holes and levers, virtually merging myself and the golden prison. Six employees scrambled from an unassuming kiosk with king-sized jars of unscented Vaseline and an enormous wooden spoon. Mighty big of them to have my favorite kind of lube, but I kind of wondered how they knew. Either way, I just couldn't wait to have that jelly saturate my skin and make me slippery enough to be birthed from this chariot.

They spent hours jamming that lube down every nook and cranny they could find. They even had me eat some hoping I would sweat it out. I accommodated like any reasonable customer would. All the while, these goddamn angels wouldn't take their eyes off of me; they didn't seem judgmental but certainly confused. Maybe they had lost their ability to judge, or maybe they were just that confused by the whole thing. Would have been nice if they had thrown a tarp on me. A man should never be forcefully pried from a chair using unscented lubricant in front of an omnipotent being. It's just common sense. I'd leave the feedback on the exit survey.

After a while, I yelled up to them and explained that I was a VIP and I was looking for my dad, but I wasn't sure they could hear me. They all just kept looking, quietly watching the pitiful struggle below. Most grew uninterested and left. Only a sparse few remained for the entirety of my glorious entrance. Eventually, my clothes were cut off of me, and one of the employees was able to slide the giant wooden spoon down my back and with enough force, they separated me from the place I had called home for the last five years. I could feel more flesh tearing as the device reluctantly relinquished my enormous body.

Holy shit! When was the last time I stood? My kneecaps moaned under the insufferable burden above and both of my legs bowed inward, threatening to snap completely. I could feel my skin wilting on the replica marble and wasn't even sure what part of me was touching it. The employees noticed my compromised state and brought over two arm crutches for me to steady myself. I could barely tell what was happening on the ground because I kept looking at the thinning crowd in the clouds and hoping to see my dad. I also wondered why I was still 50 yards from where I belonged and demanded an employee explain it to me. He nodded over to a small platform that extended from the structure like a diving board. The thing seemed an impossible distance away, even though it was probably 12–14 feet. Fourteen feet to become a god.

I put all of my weight on those damn crutches and dragged my naked body across the structure toward the platform. It must have looked pretty heroic to the holy souls above because I felt like I could hear applause, but when I looked over, I realized it was being pumped in from a Bluetooth speaker. I cursed at the employee to turn the damn thing off, told him that I didn't need some prerecorded encouragement to propel me onto that platform. Just as the thought of the bizarre applause machine crossed my mind, my arm crutches shattered underneath me, and my oiled naked body lay like a deathly overweight, jaundiced, dying, newborn baby on the marble.

The fall forced a week's worth of '50s themed human burgers and Monster Energy drinks from my bowels and onto the platform. It sprayed the white marble from my resting spot all the way to the edge of the structure. I writhed until my body had nothing left to give. It was pure ecstasy. I figured my constipation was permanent, so to see that assumption explode out of me was a hell of a relief.

This was my deliverance.

Every demon that lived inside of me was exorcised by the hand of God for the world to see, or at least the unfortunate employees standing on the structure's roof. I thought I saw the Virgin Mary in the streaks again, like I did at Auntie

Anne's, but there was no face in the mess just like there was probably no face in the half-chewed pretzel dripping down the neon menu board. The absence of a second miracle was heartbreaking. What I looked at instead was simply the boiled insides of a man finally gaining his own version of freedom. The manager's collapsed skull came to mind. Jackson Pollock came to mind. The opening in the clouds was completely empty now. Maybe I was the only one to see the beauty in the whole thing.

I yelled at the employee about the quality of the crutches and demanded they buy American next time. He assured me that this type of thing happened all the time and that I shouldn't worry. I wasn't sure what he meant, but before I could consider it too long, I heard the truck engine again. I don't care what they say, nothing sounds better than the engine of an unnecessarily large truck when you're paralyzed and helpless under the weight of your own body while desperately trying to see if your dad got his memory back in the afterlife. The next thing I knew, I felt the cool blade of the plow on my skin and my body sliding across the shit covered floor toward the platform, mopping up what it had just dispelled.

I still didn't know what the hell this platform did, but I assumed it was some kind of elevator that would finally take me to my dad— to finally let me check to make sure he was okay. Jesus, was I okay? I guess, like Jesus, I was giving my life for my dad. Sacrificing myself because I had nothing better to do. The parallel was questionable at best, but in the moment, that's what I thought.

Eventually, I had been eased onto the platform by the employee driving the F-150—what finesse! I'd let this kid plow my drive anytime. A true master of his craft. Years later, I thought I saw him plowing my neighbor's driveway, but when I waved, he acted like he didn't see me. His eyes stared vacantly forward in a desperate attempt to forget. I ended up finding his LinkedIn and endorsing him for pushing my shit-covered body across a goliath structure 50 yards away from heaven. If that doesn't get you a job, I'm not sure what does. We have enough self-appointed thought leaders and social media experts in this world; give me a guy who can glide a 500-pound man across a marble floor covered in his own excrement any day of the week.

I lay there on the platform and felt the hands of the employees wrestling with my feet. I couldn't see what they were doing over my distended stomach and bulging eyelids, but I assumed they were preparing my body for closing ceremonies, readying the elevator for its greatest task yet. It took all six of them, but they finally stood me up. I looked into the clouds and one man stood there. A single person gazing through the enormous opening to heaven. He was wearing that old Yankees cap he always did and had a newspaper under his arm with half the crossword puzzle done. He had a pencil behind his ear, and I could almost smell the black licorice gum he used to chew on his breath.

"Dad!" I yelled, "Dad!"

I was flailing my arms furiously as one of the employees tilted Monster Energy into my slackened mouth. I coughed and the nectar parted the scabs on my chin like Moses and the Red Sea. I tried calling out a few more times, but more Monster was being dumped into my mouth, prompting what felt like a seizure and a hysterical coughing fit. I doubled over and put my hands on my knees for a minute to try and catch my breath and stop dry heaving. They told me I needed my energy, so I drank as much as I could and let the rest wash over me. Several of the men steadied me, apparently preparing me for my ascension.

"I'll be right there, Dad!" I screamed through another mouthful, my eyes looking hopefully toward the clouds.

My dad seemed to wave back apathetically. I had seen that wave hundreds of times at the hospital. The polite look that accompanied his confusion. Still proudly maintaining the facade of remembering. The slight smile that one offers while passing a stranger on the street. Always putting others before himself. It was the look of someone who had lost the ability to sleep or wake. It was existing to watch TV and eat tapioca with someone you didn't know every day of the week. I wondered if it was because his spirit inhabited the afterlife as it was on earth or if he didn't recognize me. I couldn't decide which one was more upsetting, but I landed on hoping he didn't recognize me.

I had destroyed myself when no one asked me to. This wasn't a revolution or spiritual enlightenment. It was a systematic dismantling of the human spirit. I was here now, though, and there was nowhere to go but up. I'd talk to him. I'd bring him his memories in my own way. I'd make sure he was okay even when I wasn't.

"You ready?" said one of the employees in my ear.

I couldn't even talk because I was crying so hard and my throat was so raw from coughing. So I nodded at the sorry bastard and waited to be lifted into the clouds.

Instead of someone pushing a button for an elevator mechanism to painfully turn its gears and hoist me into the air, the employee in front of me, a rat-faced kid with bad acne, shoved me as hard as he could. I looked at him with confusion first and then terror and then peace. I didn't plummet immediately because my enormous body refused to give under his push, but my legs finally crumbled, and I fell off the ledge of the extended platform. I careened through the air to my certain death and I figured it was probably deserved, except dying of a heart attack in a shitty amusement park bathroom stall would have been a hell of a lot easier—and cheaper. I wondered if my dad would have been prouder of me peering up at some stranger with his pants around his ankles while my aorta exploded.

I just hoped my carcass would evaporate into the clouds before hitting the ground. Was this what happened to everyone who rode the ride? Had I paid a million dollars to suffer for five years before an assisted suicide by the hands of some poor fuck making minimum wage?

Everyone had blood on their hands, but I guess I had the most. Either way, I'd never see my dad now. Hopefully, he was alright up there. I'd finally fulfill the destiny that was laid forth by that bastard priest who was probably sipping his goddamn discounted lemonade right now. My skin was pummeled by the wind, the feeling of it slapping against itself was as painful as the gaping blisters. It folded and bent like taffy on top of itself, knotting and tangling into incomprehensible shapes. I closed my eyes and tried to think about riding the Goliath. I tried to think about those wooden beams releasing my dad's memories to him in the clouds. Maybe that roller coaster could do what I couldn't. I even thought about all of those souvenirs for a minute and then felt guilty for it because what did they matter?

The air and clouds pushed their ether rag over my mouth, and I felt a familiar unconsciousness settling in. Goddamn, this was gonna be good. I didn't fight it this time. Not even the Monster could save me from the eternal slumber that awaited, and for the first time . . . I didn't want it to.

Just as my eyelids shut, I felt a searing tear at my ankles. Both of my legs yanked with ease out of their sockets and every ligament shredded simultaneously. At least that's what it sounded like. My bones floated aimlessly inside with nothing to attach to, my knee caps in my stomach and shins in my groin. All of my skin plunged downwards while any bones fortunate enough to be connected to something pulled upwards. Every blood vessel moved painfully from my clotted arteries and was thrust into my head, which filled like a condom ready to erupt 10,000 bastard children into the world.

I could feel my ankles fasten to something and the skin around them being pulled like a piece of dried gum against an old park bench. At points, it felt like there was a single thread of skin holding onto my entire being. I vomited as I was now hurtling upwards. My skin sack changed positions once more and I began falling. My kneecaps dropped from my stomach and into my feet. After the fourth vicious cycle, I realized I wasn't dying. I was bungee jumping. Before long, I felt my body being pulled upwards, back into the clouds. I started laughing uncontrollably and then crying.

A few hours later, I felt the damp marble again on my naked body and I immediately looked into the clouds. Empty. Not a soul remained. No one cared to witness the end of my journey, not even my dad.

"Pretty rad, right?" said one of the employees, smoking a cigarette and eating a churro.

"You guys built a fucking tower, that was only 50 yards from heaven and stopped. You were 50 yards away from reuniting countless friends and family, from understanding our relationship with God and those who have passed on. Fifty yards from closure. Why the fuck did you stop? Why would you turn something with the potential to save so many into a bungee drop?" I asked, crying and out of breath. I scooped up my loose flesh in either arm and hugged it.

"I guess I never really thought about it," the employee replied without inflection. He looked up to the hole in the clouds and then back down at me and shrugged.

"We've got more customers coming through; we're gonna have to ask you to leave," he continued, sticking his hands down his pants and giving his fingers a big whiff. "Oh, I almost forgot . . ." he said, walking back over to the kiosk. He returned and presented the spoils of my descent—the treasure awarded for my annihilation. He threw a black Gildan XXXL T-shirt at me that would chafe my nipples for the next decade. It read "I survived the Afterlife" in Old English lettering. Dry clean only, he told me, but I didn't believe him. He also handed me a coupon for 20 percent off the picture of my bungee jump that I could redeem once I reached the bottom again.

"They make a killer wallet size," he said coolly. I wondered who would want to carry around a picture of themselves dangling from a bungee cord in their wallet, and then ended up buying as many as I could.

I never showed them to anyone. They sat and collected dust like the other season passes did in the box under my bed.

He flicked his cigarette over the side and before I could ask anything else, I felt the plow blade at my back once more as it began to push my broken body back down the ramp.

SIX ONE FIVE
NORTH MICHIGAN

I rode the same train every day for minutes, or days, or decades. The routine of it helped slow what would be my eventual spiral into unsalvageable madness - though finally submitting to this lunacy was the best decision I ever made, even if it was made for me. Waiting was an agreeable state for me— something that required merely a vague physical presence. Showing up and limply occupying space, existing as another benign ornament decorating the already lifeless train stop. The daily ride functioned as an anchor to reality in many ways, even though the more I rode, the less I understood. I rode not to expedite my journey, but rather to divert, or because at the time, I had nothing else to do and the train kept appearing.

The train stop was at 615 North Michigan, and as far as I knew, I was the only person ever to enter or exit the train. The placement of the stop was perplexing enough. It was an unassuming tiny room with cracking khaki walls and water-stained corners. The smell of dwindling memories and damp tiles consumed the stop, which also had an indistinct picture of a child holding a bucket. Years of wear made the image almost unintelligible, but it still functioned as a worthwhile distraction from the rest of the stop. There was nothing explicitly depressing in the room except its apparent aging.

Additionally, indeterminable neglect had left the room as faded as my gray eyes as they gazed into the foggy window that obstructed my view to an empty parking lot. Some would find no dejection in the predictable deterioration of physical objects and beings. Still, I found myself obsessed with the notion of yellowing in harmony with the shoddy drywall. The forward propulsion of mindless repetition kept me alive while also painstakingly siphoning out the slightest chance I would do anything remotely significant in my lifetime.

I would later look back on the time I squandered waiting on and riding the train and wonder if I erected an impregnable cell of insecurities from which I would die alone someday. Squandered is a relative term in this case, as the commodity of time was so worthless I had no problem burning it and warming my hands in its contaminated exhaust. Its existence functioned as more of a detriment than a commerce, and it hounded me like a shit-faced debt collector trying to repossess everything I owned. I hear the train whistle in the distance. The sound itself functioned as a key rattling in an oaken-locked door, and stirred me from the concrete mattress that my brain habitually flirted with bleeding out on.

Part of me longed to be one of the commuters that had given up on the train. Those who refused to park in the lot, wait for the sound of anguish coming from the brakes of the hulking steel bastard, or indulge in the mundanity of the train stop at all. How long had the lot been empty? How long had they stopped riding? It was possible the parking lot was not for commuters at all, rather the delusional fantasy of a budget-friendly landscaper obsessed with the perceived beauty of steaming hot asphalt. An unending moisture hanging in the recycled air of the room made it difficult to breathe. I remorsefully inhaled the beads, which sat unmoving in my chest, hugging my lungs like layers of bark on a tree and stirring a dormant panic attack from its slumber. The painting on the wall began to rattle with the train's slow ignition, as did the untold number of decorative vases filled with dying flowers that had accrued in the room. They formed a permanently grounded chandelier of thoughtless gifts, a shrine celebrating an inability to speak truth or to portray emotion. Countless presents tasked with expressing the impossible, the wilting leaves and stale water suggested failure instead of success. The rattle signified the start of the train's journey, which meant that it would still be another hour or so before boarding. It came from somewhere else. Some other room I guess. I lit a cigarette and stared at the wall of machines opposite the painting of the boy with the bucket. Unlike the painting, they never moved. Their wires and tubes formed their own ecosystem, muscle fibers, and nerves weaving in and out of the floors and walls. Fiber optic roots from an ancient oak nourishing something far more precious than they would ever know. I stare at the black hole where they all seemed to converge, an abyss hurtling toward the inevitable.

There were undoubtedly other things on the train, but nothing like me. Nothing was composed of anything as frustrating as flesh and blood, both of which were constructed to fail—and I endlessly worried about that failure. The train's liveliness juxtaposed the deadness of the waiting room, suggesting they were not related at all, often making me feel as though I was never meant to ride the train. The lumbering steel carriage and I seemed indifferent to each other's being. We both realized the relationship was transactional in nature, me paying in more ways than I could have ever imagined. It followed no schedule from what I could tell, which would have been a frustrating nuance for a mode of transportation, but outside of the brief journey, my days were filled with staring at a dark mass of blankets that struggled to warm my thinning limbs beneath it. The unnaturally black cocoon grew darker by the day.

The train's whistle blows again, belching its presence into the weighty air and destroying the rhythmic sonar's strangle-like hold on a room gasping for breath. Then quiet. The sonar re-establishes its voice; its haunting Morse code homily longs for something even more monotonous yet. The gnarled orgy of blankets seems to stir, but I confuse actual movement with the slow drip of a water pouch hanging from one of the machines. Not yet. I look at my watch, the arthritic second hand moved with obvious pain, laboring under the weight of human desire. I have waited longer than I ever have before. It has never been this late, though I hastily apply the construct of punctuality to just about anything—even objects that are entirely unaware of any expectation. I demanded adherence to my imaginary rule set as a distraction and the train was coming dangerously close to betrayal.

I often wondered how the train ran. Who funded the train? What entity steered its rusted wheels? Did it have a purpose outside of precariously balancing my sanity? Maybe I entertained these questions as an additional diversion from the sadness that had recently found refuge within the friendly confines of my being. The notion of a train without an objective, save my aimless journey, created a dull paranoia that enjoyed a prosperous marriage with sadness. Sipping tea and comfortably growing old while I desperately sought a method for eviction.

The train's whistle screams once more, now creating an unmistakable disturbance in the melancholy nest. I light another cigarette and the beeping in the room ceases. It is wholly quiet at the train stop. The silence pushes the smoke back into my agape mouth, and the fumes burrow enthusiastically into my capillaries. They retreat further still. My heart beats in my ears, stomach, and toenails.

I drop the cigarette onto the floor and quietly suffocate it with the toe of my shoe. My favorite part. The impending death rattle that would eventually birth life back into the dying womb that had kept us involuntarily together for so long. First, the uneasy groaning of the walls as the organ meat of the room begins expanding, preparing itself. The ribcage of beams and tiles bow to accommodate the ballooning features of the room. I step back and fall nonchalantly into a rocking chair I have fallen into hundreds of times before. Inexplicably, it is the only thing not moving, not cracking. An assumption of motion accompanies its curved legs; they lack the will or capacity to rock anymore. Perhaps unhappy with the predisposed conjecture, it quietly protests its sole purpose. Its modest protest provides calm during the chaotic transformation. Aged mahogany with the smell of fresh varnish and my fingers seek the familiar wounds in the wood to warm themselves further before the train's arrival. I don't recall the origin of that habit and its peculiarity isn't lost on me, but the absentminded indulgence is a necessary part of the ritual. The inside of the wood is unexpectedly warm.

Next, the feverish shaking, the shattering of fluorescent lights, and the razing of the entire room. It always appears similar the next day, but for now, there is nothing. Myself and the bed. The sheets and eventually the featureless pale face, which would offer the train from its impossibly small mouth. I learned to cherish the moment immediately before the journey, taking comfort in the dichotomy between chaos and silence. I often found it was the only thing that could pry me from the depths of purposeless forward momentum, a forced reflection. The whistle blows once again and a dull glow begins to slowly form several feet in front of me. Its movements are similar to a mason jar of fireflies suspended by a bowing fishing line. I had fantasized about making something similar as a child, but there were no fireflies in my hometown and the time spent on creating such an elaborate lamp was counterintuitive to how carefree I was at the time. Nowadays, I worship the prospect of toiling away at something so frivolous. Obsess over every detail as a vacation of sorts and eventually create something I love but ultimately designate as waste, deposit the jar full of dead fireflies and simple fishing pole into the tide of a forgotten trash vortex already ripe with my creations.

As minutes, hours, or even days pass, the glow grows in size, bobbing methodically in the somber room, tilting from side to side as though determining my worthiness as a passenger. As though this was my first time riding. As though it had never seen me before. As though there is some inescapable denial. Eventually, when close enough, the luminosity unveils its final form. Placement of barely visible lines in the otherwise unnaturally smooth exterior would suggest a human face, or at least something once human. I wonder if I am projecting humanity onto the object to normalize the otherwise uncanny aura, but the lines seem more real than not. The lines were deeper once. Maybe when I first started riding. The light in the room clusters into varying pockets in a seeming attempt to manifest something ambiguously human. It mimics something it once saw, trying to breathe life into a collapsing memory.

An unidentifiable familiarity seems to be deteriorating with each ride. In some ways, I found the smoothed face more pleasant to look at, easier to digest, to comprehend. In other ways, its imprecision filled me with undirected concern and disgust for its willingness to alter the essence of what it once was. It exchanged perceivable shadows and wrinkles for a characterless orb state, and I wondered if the trade was consensual.

Egg-shaped, the vacant eyes peer forward, and the pupils are noticeably absent. The milky sockets rotate states of sopping wet and severe dryness in no particular interval until, finally, a hole opens in the lower half of the face and a train glides effortlessly into the room. The train's wheels and carriage inherit a lubricant from their source— something that I approached with unbridled skepticism on my first few rides, but had now become another facet of my ever-growing ritual. I run my hands across the glossy exterior. The lubricant peels under my hands, molting onto the floor like dead skin. Some of the material seems to melt directly into my palms, making them as smooth as the face itself before receding back to their worn actuality.

My fingers search resolutely for the almost microscopic lever that would open the doors to the train car. Finally, I find it. The location of the lever seems to change with every ride, but there was never any threat of the train departing without me. Even if I don't find it, the train doors always open. My search and eventual entry invariably depend on my fluctuating eagerness or readiness. The train always waits. A small game played between myself and the object I had grown to love. The inexplicable standoff always satisfied both participants. It wants me to ride. I want to ride. The pulling of the lever, with a texture and weight of wet leaves, was a mere formality in a foregone agreement, an unspoken promise to one another. Even on days of transcendent reluctance, when the doors opened, I dutifully boarded. On those days, the trip seemed longer than ever. There was an urgency in its motion on those days, a sad but unnecessary desperation to prove its capability. I never gave its willingness or ability much thought, but the concept of a train's diminishing perception of itself was heart-breaking and confusing.

I looked behind the train as I sometimes did. A morbid curiosity about the condition of whatever it was that had fashioned the train. The face, as it was, sat in a deflated heap, tilted downwards and sagging heavily, yearning for the floor below. The lips of the train hole slackened to the point of actually touching the cracking tiles of the stop itself. The slumped nature of the skin like the slack of the face would suggest exhaustion, but upon closer inspection, it was unquestionably apathetic. The apparent disinterest conveyed by the shape the deadened eyes had taken was unsettling, given the achievement accomplished. I had the sudden urge to hold the cold-looking face, console it, though it demanded no consolation or warm words.

Conversely, the blackness of the hole begged me to join the face in its mood of indifference. Each of us assigned sympathy toward each other's respective perceived plight: caring and uncaring, neither acting on the desire at hand. Our collective compassion never breached the tenuous threshold for action. We remained passive observers without will. The relaxed face was hypnotizing, and I craved a morsel of further scrutiny, but the whistle blew once more. I could sense the impatience of the unknown conductor responsible for propulsion.

The doors shut immediately behind me and I sat down on

one of the sloped mounds, which looked and felt like taffy. The warmth of the substance suggested a prior occupant, but the cabin was as deserted as ever. I still can't shake the feeling that someone was there or even still was. I always seem to just miss someone… The immovable proximity toward fulfillment instills crippling helplessness. Uncontrollable and unpredictable circumstances dictated by a lunatic conductor. A conductor whom I was growing resentful of, questioning its judgment and capacity to execute the duties necessary to be a conductor. Whatever force was pummeling this train farther into oblivion sought to deprive me of a validation I badly needed—that I was not the only passenger.

Nevertheless, I rode. I had to know why. Years of senseless riding and gorging on structured pageantry had led me here. Sitting numbly in a pre-warmed seat and finally considering the catalyst of our relationship. Why had it started? What had fueled its longevity? Was there an ending?

The cabin was lined with thousands of tiny glassless windows. Their abundance and depth resembled an intricate system of glands and pores used for the cooling and filtration of a living organism. As far as I could tell, they do nothing for the train, a mere celebration of impractical décor inconveniencing something pursuing complete anonymity. Their volume and symmetry are remarkable, but it ends there. I want them to explain why I am here, or at least function as something more than an inadequate glimpse to the outside world, but they are just holes, and their triviality is maddening. The once charming cavities now reminded me of the neglected sponge occupying my kitchen sink, and I can almost smell the earthy film bleeding from every nook and cranny of its many crevices. Their size makes it impossible to see outside of the train and I grow more vexed at the blatant disobedience for which a window is traditionally created.

I light another cigarette.

It has never been unequivocally stated if smoking is a permitted pastime, but I have avoided reprimand up to this point. Burning the first cigarette all of those years ago on this train was a risk unlike any other. What a win that was. What an accomplishment. I celebrated that pathetic moment of significance for years to come before finally realizing the celebration had transformed into a ruthless obsession with the drink that eventually destroyed everything I loved. I still didn't know what that life looked like. I only knew this ride.

There has never been glass in those diminutive windows and the night air carries in the distant smell of burning ethanol. Through the obstructed honeycomb of holes, I can see the train slowly beginning to move back into the face. Without a sound. My eyes are drawn to the mouth of the face gasping for air. Its pained inhalations summon the train, which feverishly abides. Numerous times the face fails to generate enough breath for motion, but eventually, it gains speed with each short breath, before finally succumbing to a baptism in nothingness. I take another puff of my cigarette, but it's only filter, so I shove it into one of the holes. The filter shrivels into dust and empties into the greedy lungs of the night air. My meager offering seems to satisfy the evening abyss. Though not my original intent, I feel happy with my small contribution of garbage to the unknown ecosystem.

I peer over my shoulder, confirm the company of a small, dated camera suspended by flesh-like threads growing from the ceiling, and I begin to reconsider my initial diagnosis of the windows. When I first noticed the brutal red pupil dissecting my insides years ago, I met its probing gaze with understandable suspicion. Any feeling toward it has since disappeared. Now, the light wasn't on, and the former glory held by the piercing red light was simply reduced to wilted burgundy. The tired transformation reminds me of the face. Either the batteries ran out or whoever presided over the camera decided there was nothing worth recording. I assumed without hesitation the latter. A solitary beige mass enjoying the complete absence of motion was a triumph unworthy of observation. There was nothing to do with any of the tapes anyways. No one to share them with. They are probably used as fuel to keep this thing running. Simply someone who was tolerating a perpetual state of stagnation aboard a train hurdling nowhere in particular. Maybe prior passengers warranted surveillance; maybe I was once as interesting as they were. However, the sheer willingness of someone to endure this day after day would suggest a deficiency in noteworthy hobbies. Anyone willing to entertain an obsession with such an unrelentingly mundane obligation surely had nothing left to give.

I turn back around and stare forward at the rest of the empty train car. It is only a matter of time before the gnawed gum interior awakens. I think the heat coming from the fluorescent lighting activates it and then I second-guess myself. An oppressive hue feebly drizzling from an oblong bulb could never inspire the wealth of emotion that lurked in the seams of the sinewy floorboards. That type of light was reserved as a tranquilizer for already sleepy executives after masturbating onto a stack of unreadable pie charts. It fed off the paralyzed losers shitting their ill-fitting pants in a five-hour strategy meeting. It was designed to burn brighter as hope and inspiration slowly bled out, and it drew its life from the translucent skin of the melting disciples who had no choice but to worship at its altar day after day. Not this one. This string of lights created something otherworldly. I didn't think a fluorescent light was capable of creating something so beautiful until riding the train.

I glance down at my phone and observe thousands of missed calls, texts, and emails. A cruel red pin adheres to each of the insufferable modes of communication. Taunting numbers and their red bulbs bloat in an effort to emphasize disappointment. They beg to be split open and lapped up, bitten into and choked down, spat back up, and force-fed to the next unwilling participant in the cascading pyramid of pointless correspondence. I think of the rocking chair and refuse.

The floor begins to spiral and I realize the start of the parade looms. I deemed it a parade because there wasn't really another word for it. The procession of eccentric happenings was always the same and it seemed like a celebration of sorts. Some facets resembled a heavily distorted commemoration, memories—but not. Because it happened every day, there was no correlation with any calendar holiday. I decided to abandon any contemplation in favor of just watching. Something about this moment suggested it required commitment to memory, a momentary break from the unquestioning completion of tasks. The floor turns from taffy to cotton candy moss, brightly colored and covered in white strings that tremble in the cabin air. Slowly, the strings adjourn their seemingly arbitrary motion, favoring instead a complex cycle of extending and intertwining. As the ligaments continue to grow, rip, rebuild, and fuse, I stare at the frenzied construction and cannot fully realize the complexity and synchrony. I begin to cry as the unusual threads weave their story.

A father teaching his son to grill on an antique lamp

A tiger made of marbles devouring a flesh flower

A record player spinning the sounds of human hair

A glass trampoline

A lamb smeared with mint jelly gumdrops

A gambler losing everything

An abandoned campsite with a dead comedian

A swimming pool full of pulled teeth

A rat servant reciting names of people who had died in the war

A mason jar of circus peanuts

The best Christmas tree

A hot air balloon fueled by the cigarette smoke of sinners

A tiny spider city

An owl with the face of a hound and the body of an ex-
lover

An unopened letter from 50 years ago

A boy knitting an oversized quilt

A seafood tower of Polaroid pictures

A nail technician giving a manicure to a blade of grass

A bottle of Jack Daniels trying to save its family

A watermelon full of cactus needles

An ice sculpture rosary

A hospital bed

A television set

Incomprehensible emotions working in unison to prove
that it wasn't over, that they weren't done yet. Not ready
to give. Not yet, at least. In that ephemeral moment, they
appeared incapable of letting me down.

"He won't remember any of this?" I ask the man in the
white coat, tears continuing to stream down my face. He
doesn't reply, but the gentle squeeze on my shoulder
indicates he doesn't have to. We both understood. Him
sooner than me, and I begin to cry again.

Big! ELECTION! DAY!

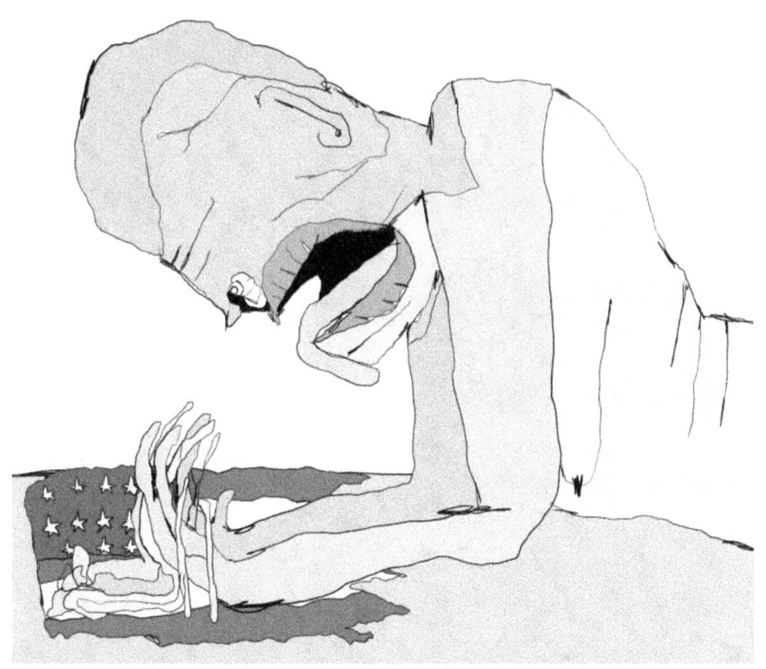

Election day was his favorite day, though it sometimes spanned days or even months. The boy had never experienced the electoral college or a voting process with multiple polling places spanning across every state. Pundits with no particular credentials or education had called it the great streamlining of modern democracy on varying indistinguishable television shows. They sipped their thermoses of grain alcohol and laughed at each others' jokes until their veneers fell out and their tonsils bled.

No one was quite sure where the new election process was born, but historians pointed back to episode 243 of *America's Got Talent* when an inbred ostrich farmer dressed in drag overdosed on heroin and got a standing ovation from the judges and the audience. After the doctors injected his heart with adrenaline to revive him, he grabbed the microphone and predicted a future where the entire country descended on a single town to determine the next president. He died moments after and received another standing ovation, though he didn't end up winning the season. The winner of that particular season went to a man who had his arms replaced by chainsaws and did magic tricks on a flaming dirt bike.

Now every four years, the voters traveled from near and far to South Bend, Indiana, to cast their vote for the candidate they thought most qualified to run the country further into the ground. Some refused, calling the voting process unconstitutional while others called it quintessentially American. Whatever the opinion, reality was a singular, seemingly unending line that spanned the entire city. Once the line reached the end, the election was considered over, and a winner was declared. Some questioned why an uninspiring town in northern Indiana was picked as the destination for something so momentous. The only logical explanation was the wide variety of abandoned warehouses to choose as the official polling place. That combined, of course, with the availability of heroin, an abundance of strip malls, and the proximity to the world's largest recreational vehicle museum. It contained attractions or activities for virtually anyone visiting the city, from any walk of life.

The city did its part to appear festive by painting the streets as American flags and building effigies of former presidents out of asbestos. Some houses hung Christmas lights and others reenacted the Civil War. Most sat in their front lawns and reverently observed the monotony of the line. Many out-of-town people turned the occasion into an extended vacation, a perfect realization of civic duty and depressing family time.

They let their kids take pictures next to dying goats at the Potawatomi petting zoo and got them overpriced souvenirs from the University of Notre Dame bookstore. They would eat undercooked chicken at Bar Louie and barely tip servers. Sometimes parents would treat themselves to a Segway tour of a Chrysler dealership or a few gallons of Long Island iced tea from the Linebacker Lounge before driving home drunk. Driving drunk was a favorite local pastime that election tourists also grew to love. Something about blowing through a stop sign while vomiting out of the driver's side window onto a raccoon corpse had a fairy tale's makeup. Swerving in and out of traffic as they wrestled with consciousness was nirvana; it proved they loved country and family. It was more dangerous to not be drunk on the road on any given night in South Bend—at least that was the rationalization most made.

Most kids would resent Notre Dame for the rest of their lives, the four-leaf clover serving as a beacon for pain and suffering during those holidays. Parents came away with their own souvenirs, something to cherish the remainder of the uneventful year. A patch with a tiny American flag and the phrase, "I voted" was sewn onto their foreheads until it was scraped off four years later and replaced with a new one. The crude display of perceived patriotism was a badge of honor, a replacement for a personality, and perpetual proof of undying sophistication. It was something to talk about instead of the weather. The chewed skin that never seemed to fully heal asserted their ability to follow directions. Sometimes they paired this with a stolen bar of Irish Spring soap from the Wooden Indian Motel while the maids washed blood from the sheets.

People who didn't visit the city to vote attempted to manufacture counterfeit patches, but there was an unmistakable look in their eye that they hadn't experienced the wonders of northern Indiana. Maybe it was lingering happiness or the fact that the sulfurous air from neighboring Gary, Indiana, hadn't permanently embedded in their skin. Maybe they just appeared intangibly less American.

When he was younger, the boy would set up a popcorn stand and sell tiny Ziploc bags for a quarter to people who waited in line. His parents would also sell parking spots on their lawn for $20. He loved that their yard was a temporary home for voters. Although the grass would be ruined and their yard would be an unredeemable slop pit of mud and garbage, it was worth it for the few hundred dollars and the privilege of hosting the voters. His family would spend the weeks after the election picking up unspeakable human filth. The boy remembered finding a bird that had choked to death on a bottle cap. They later had a funeral for the bird and his mom told him that it died doing what it loved. He wouldn't ever grasp what she meant by it, but in the moment, it comforted him. He cried himself to sleep that night, all for a bird he never knew. He wondered if choking was really what it loved.

He would bundle up and play football with his brother, sometimes passing the ball to people in line and running as far as he could to receive their passes, which oftentimes fell depressingly short. He would scoop the ball from the cold grass and jog it to the next person in line until he was called in for supper and a hot bath before bed. Fall in South Bend meant burning leaves and jumping in leaf piles; it meant layering, hooded sweatshirts, wool socks, hot coffee, hot apple cider, football, the smell of cigars, and mustard; it meant soccer chairs and tailgating for things he didn't care about.

Maybe it was fall he loved more than the election, but they became one in his mind because they corresponded. When he was very young, he would ask his parents every year why there weren't visitors, unable to comprehend that it happened only every four years. His parents once held a fake election for him when he was particularly distraught, which delighted him to no end. They stood in a line outside of the house and took turns entering while the boy dutifully counted ballots. At the end of the night, they all ate mom's famous chicken kiev casserole and playfully argued if the ballots were counted correctly, to which the boy said he would never betray the sanctity of the process. He slept without dreaming that night.

When he was old enough, he fantasized about participating in the ritual. He saw the look of pride from people exiting the abandoned warehouse and wondered what it must feel like to control the entire country's destiny. The responsibility seemed unimaginable to him and sometimes he found himself wondering if he was worthy of such a decision. These were heroes he looked at in line, though they didn't resemble those in the comic books he loved. Many appeared purposefully in opposition to the body types and chiseled faces he was accustomed to. His dad had explained that heroes come in all shapes and sizes, and the boy nodded.

The boy was lucky enough to grow up in that town and even luckier yet to live only blocks from the abandoned warehouse in which votes were cast. At one point he and his brother bought a video camera and microphone to host their very own election day home video show. They walked up and down the enormous line intending to interview anyone who was willing to talk to them. He remembered asking his parents if they thought he and his brother would make it on the local news. His mom tousled his hair and told him anything was possible.

"We're reporting live from the line in South Bend, Indiana. Which candidate are you voting for?" the boy asked a portly man with bowed legs and palpable indigestion.

"Have you considered killing yourself?" said the man, returning to his phone.

The boys ran to the next person in line. A liver spotted

elderly woman who smelled like wet hay.

"What happens inside the warehouse?" asked the boy.

"Something special. Though, I fear this will be my last year voting," she responded, coughing blood into a tissue before issuing them a hard candy that they reluctantly accepted.

The boy would never forget the way her hands shook or the rope-like veins that protruded from every thinning layer of skin. The hard candy was eaten on a dare years later, having the essence of a dog rawhide and ACE bandage.

They never saw the woman again but convinced themselves she was always hidden somewhere in the line.

After two interviews, they grew bored and gave up. They dropped the camera in the entry hall to their house and never picked it up again. The footage was erased eventually and replaced with the boy's high school graduation, which was also never watched again. They would repeat this with piano, soccer, clarinet, woodworking, and just about every activity their parents dumped money into. It wasn't that they weren't grateful, they just couldn't find what they were looking for. Maybe they knew that deep down, they weren't meant to excel at anything. Maybe it was a restlessness for escape before they could wrap their heads around the concept of being trapped.

The length of the line itself was incredible, it went as far as his eyes could see and then some. Sometimes he selfishly wondered if waiting that long was worth it, but immediately reminded himself that the fate of the country was at stake. His dad had made sure he knew this. From a very young age, they were taught that voting might be the most important thing they do in their lives. Maybe this was the reason they quit everything. Though it was more likely that they simply didn't pride themselves on suffering through things like previous generations. They opted for comfort and convenience instead of painstaking, pointless devotion.

His fascination with the election and the line itself waned over the years, though he still found himself hypnotized by the immensity of the line and the voters' resolve. He and his brother grew apart for no reason in particular. Sometimes they would talk about the time they tried to interview people in line and laugh at how embarrassing the prospect was. They promised to call each other more but never did. They planned game nights and complained about the obligation until a last-minute, sorrowful cancellation was offered with a promise to eventually reschedule.

After the boy graduated high school, he did what most people did: signed up for sports management classes at the community college for a degree he would never finish for a profession that didn't exist. He worked at University Park Mall on the side and got drunk as hell with other friends who would never leave. Sometimes they slept with high schoolers they bought beer for. They were all dying under the faint glow of the garage refrigerator light but lived like kings who presided over an empire of melting snow mounds and liver failure. Their distorted reality was held loosely together by the resin scraped from varying weed smoking devices and the bacon grease they threw in their front yard.

They threw house parties and smoked menthol cigarettes inside and posted boastful pictures wearing flat-brimmed hats. He tried heroin once because it was around, but it made him throw up, and he felt guilty for months. He never tried it again and, at that moment, was thankful for the Irish Catholic guilt that dictated almost every other aspect of his life. He recalled his second-grade teacher telling him that every time he sinned, it was like nailing another barb into Jesus on the cross, and he wondered how deep he had driven that needle into the limp feet of his savior.

They sometimes traveled to Michigan for vacation and got just as drunk there, posting pictures of themselves drinking domestic beers by the lake with the hashtag #PureMichigan. They knew every bar deal in town on any given night and sometimes got free appetizers at Olive Garden. The sack of stale bread sticks and jars of expired marinara served as reminders of royalty.

The boy and his friends never missed a Notre Dame home game and they would remind anyone of this. Their infantile obsession with a university that was unaware of their existence was all they had. They cheered on the team as though they were brothers and got so drunk at their tailgate that all conversation would cease. The group was seen as an embarrassment by every other tailgate and the hordes of elitist alumni, but they maintained that their allegiance to Notre Dame was something they were born with instead of bought. Graduating from the university itself was an unnecessary formality in the undying quest to get loaded and have unprotected sex in a truck bed filled with Natural Ice. They wore the same quarter-zip sweaters and brunch boots as the other alumni and students who were equally insufferable.

No one lived like they did, at least as far as they knew. Their lifestyle was fueled by the insular nature of their friendships and the sad women they slept with. When people who had left the city came back to visit, he and his friends sneered and laughed at them because they were dumb enough to leave. It didn't matter what city they left for or what job they took. By moving, they betrayed their hometown and, in doing so, forsook those who stayed. They betrayed the unsaid pact of unemployment, alcoholism, and poverty. Those people were viewed as inferior in every way: They had lost the pulse of the city whose heart barely beat anyways. They would never go to as many football games as they did or drink as many beers on any given weeknight. They sold out when the boy and his friends refused, even if that refusal wasn't their choice and meant stagnating their lives in the pool of hardened Jagermeister that was caked onto the bottom of their coffee table.

The city gnawed away at him like it did all of its residents. Used his bones and flesh as mortar for another payday loan store. Burned his hopes and dreams to aid in its digestion of other residents and fuel to heat more heroin spoons. Washed him down its phlegm-ridden throat with another generous gulp from its polluted river.

On a rainy day in early November, he got a call from his parents. He had turned 23 months earlier and had spent the last quarter celebrating the passive achievement. The previous night was spent at the Glow Worm, where the boy and his friends casually drank *White Russians* while quoting *The Big Lebowski* in favor of having actual conversations. They got lap dances from women that were more OxyContin than human and complained to the manager about the quality of the strippers and what they felt they were entitled to. They themselves acted and resembled something that didn't render on the evolution spectrum. Their inexcusable behavior was justified by designating the club as 'a piece of shit,' even though they had been there every week in the last month.

That piece of shit had been reheated and snorted greedily with stepped-on coke, ground up in a pepper cracker onto sweaty microwaved dinners. That piece of shit embraced them in its steaming hot coils when no one else would, suffocating them in its unending girth. Although they lived in the city and were a portrait of its backward residents in many ways, they resented the very parts of the town that lived inside of them. They were contemptuous of the awful bars and restaurants even though they were the best the city could offer, even though they didn't deserve better.

He was hungover as a bastard but answered the call anyway. He knew that if he didn't, it would haunt every conversation for the next month. He would be shamed and ostracized, placed under the brutal scrutiny of his father's microscope, and forced to pay back the debt with a flurry of feigned interest in varying family matters for months. Not answering was not an option.

"Son, it's time for you to come home," said the father forebodingly.

The boy's heart sank. His mind combed through a Rolodex

containing every imaginable opportunity for disappointment, wondering which card his father would pull. The father was constantly pulling, sometimes faster than he could fill it. He could always feel his father's fingers dancing gleefully over his growing collection of regret.

The boy laughed. "What do you mean, Dad?" he asked nervously.

"The election is only three days away and you can finally vote," said the dad placidly.

The boy hadn't thought about politics in years. He hadn't thought a lot about anything. Many of his memories were pissed into the ice-filled trough at Corby's Bar & Grill, melting into the neglected South Bend sewer system with thousands of other recollections and bowel evacuations from other drunks. He remembered rare moments of drunken clarity standing at the urinals. Sometimes when the piss was extra long, it afforded him the time for self-reflection, which was retreated from in favor of soaking the paper towel dispenser with his dehydrated yellow stream. He would come back to his friends, sometimes morose, but was offered a shot and a cigarette and gladly sunk back into the realm of unthinking the city provided him.

Other memories weren't worth storing at all, even for a moment. They were either unworthy, or he was incapable. Both prospects saddened him. He began to wonder why he seemed to remember things from his childhood more than he did in the last five years. He wondered if it was because milestones didn't exist anymore. There were no great achievements or celebrations anymore. Unable to find a stud, it was impossible for anything to hang. Even things that seemed important at the time dangled from loose nails that would dislodge with every door closure. Without those anchors, memories drifted freely in and out of his head and were eventually cast far enough out to completely forget. Where had all of the ballasts gone? Without anyone serving him those formative memories, he was starving. Every significant moment in his life had been a consequence of someone else's prescription.

First Communion. Graduation. Confirmation. Graduation. Getting a job. Losing a job. Succumbing to alcoholism, though he would never admit that.

He had no capacity to create his own, no way of tying a knot to any of the anchors he carelessly hoisted overboard. All he could do was watch the bubbles release from his empty indulgences as they plummeted to the seafloor.

He always remembered the line, though. The vividness at which it came back was incredible. The fake interviews, playing catch with strangers, his brother, and the sense of duty his dad instilled in him.

"Mom and I were thinking you come back home for a few days, enjoy the election festivities like we all used to," continued the dad calmly.

Something about the summons was heartbreaking. Maybe it was the delirium caused by his hangover, but the somber invitation made him want to cry. In that moment, there seemed to be a shared longing for the boy he once was. He could tell his parents needed him and he needed them.

"Sure, Dad, that sounds great," said the boy, fighting back the tears.

He convinced himself that the hangover had created that momentary vulnerability, but deep down, he knew he needed to go home. The ironic part was, home was only several blocks from his house, but there was something different about staying instead of visiting as well as something different in his dad's voice.

Later that day, he packed a bag and traveled to his childhood home. He planned to stay at his parents' house for two days and then get in line to finally place his vote. Something he had dreamt about for years, forgotten about, and was now the only thing driving him. It was good to have purpose, even if that vocation was standing in line for several days before casting an ill-informed vote for someone on the verge of a mental collapse. The boy viewed it as a redemption opportunity of sorts, something he would remember the rest of his life. He couldn't wait to see his parents, stand in line, and soak in the sacred tradition of it all.

His mom and dad greeted him as he pulled into the driveway; the rest of the yard was already full of cars from election tourists. He couldn't believe that the occasion had slipped entirely from his mind; bars around the city had been unusually full. Their collapsing rafters propped up by the laughter and livelihood of fresh blood. The corpse of the city would be loaded into a wheelchair and pushed around for the next few days. City officials would apply makeup to its jaundiced face and have it wear a fancy hat to distract visitors from its protruding ribs and withering arms. It would be force-fed enough prescription pills to mimic rudimentary human emotions. Cheap perfume would cover the stench of wound rot, and the voters would be unaware of the city's looming and inevitable collapse. Once the election was over, the city would immediately resume its vegetative state.

The boy had sensed the frenzy, but was too stuck in his own haze to notice South Bend experiencing the false rebirth it did every four years. After the election was over, the city would be put back to sleep like the residents at Manorcare Nursing Home, with a damp ether rag and a steaming mug of skim milk.

That night his mom made her famous Chicken Kiev casserole for them. His brother couldn't come back, since he had moved down south and had a family. The boy was disappointed as the dinner conversation ran in unison with the stuffing streaming slowly from his dried chicken breast.

"You look thin," said the mom, tilting her head slightly and looking sympathetically at the boy.

It was the last thing he wanted to hear, as though weight fluctuation somehow dictated mental and physical health. There was no response to the conjecture either, even if he had or hadn't lost any weight. There was nothing to say. He nodded and joked, "It's because I'm not eating great meals like this!"

In actuality, the meal wasn't great. It wasn't like he remembered. The hormone ripe chicken breast, which was the size of a catcher's mitt, was incinerated. Its grayish meat tattered with every painful cut, little white calluses, and tags clustered around enormous tendons. The vegetables were canned or frozen or both, inheriting the worst properties from either undesirable state. He reflected on the fake election day his parents hosted when he was a child and remembered it being the best meal of his life. Was that memory incorrect? Embellished? He pushed it around his plate and looked up every now and again to catch a corner of his mom's caring eyes. They wanted desperately for him to like what was on his plate, to love the people he was sitting across from.

She had put everything she had into this awful dinner. Into recreating that special moment they shared all of those years ago. Something about her heart and soul being piledrived into a barely thawed chicken breast and baked in the oven they hadn't cleaned in decades made his eyes well up. It made him feel unworthy and embarrassed, guilty for not coming around more. It wasn't a lot, but it was a lot for her. A microwaved spring vegetable medley bag was her way of showing she cared.

The hardened peas and carrots were somehow a gift unlike any other. They sat on his plate like flesh carved from her thinning frame.

The boy welled up once more.

He smiled at her and she smiled back at him as he politely finished every last bite. The boy knew a stomach ache was coming, anticipated lying in his old twin bed and fluctuating between hot and cold all night. It was worth it to prove his love, to prove that he hadn't changed and that they could still have nights like they had when he was a kid. He just hoped that the meat would leave his system before he got in line.

After several more hours at the table, the family exhausted every inconsequential topic of conversation. They discussed Netflix shows, the weather, a neighbor that he didn't know had died, and the new beige paint applied to the bathroom. When they had no mundane observations left to give, they cleared the table quietly. The mom said she had a headache and was going to lie down early. The boy said he wasn't tired yet and got a light beer from the fridge. He sat in the backyard and listened to his neighbor's labored breaths while he smoked a cigarette. The emphysema cut through the night air, advertising to the neighborhood that he was slowly dying. They could both hear the indistinguishable chatter of the line as it breached their block of houses, which was about two miles from the abandoned warehouse where the voting would begin the next morning.

"Cold out tonight," said the neighbor to the boy, his face obscured by a grapevine that hadn't produced anything for years.

The neighbor's usual primary point of conversation was around the most recent misfortune that afflicted him and his family. It was an endless list of oddities, unimaginable that they would happen to anyone at all, let alone all happening to one person. Though in some ways, the boy thought he existed because of these afflictions, that without them, he would have nothing at all. His entire life was spent correcting cosmic inconveniences and wrestling with his tainted kismet. He told the stories of financial loss and personal injury with an uncanny pride.

"Definitely," said the boy, taking a sip out of his beer.

He wasn't in the mood for talking; he wanted to listen to the strangers in the line. He had gone to sleep to those voices so many times as a child. Those were the best nights of sleep of his life that he remembered. He hoped that hadn't changed too, like so much else had already changed.

"You gonna vote?" asked the neighbor, taking another long drag from his cigarette and following it with an immense coughing fit.

"I am," said the boy, "Are you?"

"Last time I voted, I got a damn worm," said the neighbor with a slight chuckle. The boy didn't care to ask if this was a metaphor or reference to an actual parasite that still lived inside of him.

"I'm done with voting, I'll be watching the results on my new flat-screen TV. Took out a second mortgage for it, but it's got the best pixel ratio on the market!"

The neighbor took another long pause, perhaps waiting for the boy to react to his new luxury entertainment system, and the courage it took to live outside of his means. Instead, the boy sat silent, wondering who would inherit the neighbor's debts once he finally passed.

"Knudson better damn well win it this year or this country is in for hell," said the neighbor, dropping his cigarette and snuffing it out with one of his gas station flip-flops. "Anyways, good talking!"

The boy listened to the sound of his flip-flops as he walked back up his porch and disappeared into his ranch-style home. Just as the neighbor vanished into his consumerist abyss to enjoy an evening with his prized television, the boy heard the familiar sound of their back screen door opening. His dad popped his head with two more beers dangling between his fingers. He raised them slightly, and the boy nodded at the silent gesture, an agreement to the dad's moderate offering. The dad grabbed a seat near the boy, a rusting, wrought iron chair that had plagued the family with its discomfort since the boy was little. His parents refused to get rid of it, a testament to their Midwestern obsession with waste and settling with what they already had. The boy appreciated this about his parents: Their aversion to luxury was in stark contrast to the neighbor, but sometimes their avoidance of convenience or comfort saddened him. They deserved everything, but for some reason, battled the numb legs and sore lower back inflicted by the chair.

"You ready for tomorrow?" asked the dad, quietly twisting the top off of his beer and throwing the cap into the yard.

"I think so," said the boy. "I was actually thinking about going out there tonight . . . you know get a jump on things."

"That so?" asked the dad, taking another sip from his beer. "Sick of me and your mom already?"

"No!" the boy blurted out immediately after the question was asked. "It's just that, I don't want to be too far back in the line. This is just a really big moment in a lot of ways for me," he stammered, hoping that the immediacy of his response would diffuse the barbed accusation.

"I'm just kidding. I know it is. I think you should do it. If that's what your gut is telling you, get into that line and get that vote in," said the dad. "I was hoping we could all wait in line together, but I remember my first time voting, and it was my moment alone, so I understand."

Relieved, the boy sat back in his chair. He looked at the bottle in his hand and realized his beer was already almost empty. He couldn't believe how fast he drank sometimes. The pace of consumption was crafted and honed like an ancient swordsmith. Years of beginning every night with the sole intention of pants-shitting annihilation. There was no cherishing of moments, no natural flow to any given evening. Every night simply served as another opportunity to forget the piece of shit life he constructed. His memory mopped up stale beer and half drank cocktails before being mercifully rung into his clogged shower drain. He never really owned them; they belonged to the drink, the drain, and the city. On some lucky mornings, he could reflect on them briefly as they sat stagnantly in the nest of hair in the drain, but eventually, they were pulled into the rusted pipes and never thought of again. He was a beast of burden for the drink, which rode him into the pavement any night it could.

"Think it might be time," he said to his dad, tilting the empty bottle at him.

The dad nodded, with a subtle disapproval that the boy could still distinguish. They both got up and walked back through the house toward the front door. The dad had packed a cooler for the boy and included a sleeping bag, as no one was ever quite certain how many hours or days the line would bleed from them.

"This was the same sleeping bag I used when I cast my first vote, same with the cooler," said the dad proudly.

The small accumulation of items sent the boy spiraling again. It wasn't much, but it was everything. The cooler's size in particular saddened the boy as did the look of satisfaction on the dad's face at the pile of things they had kept all of those years. Proudly stored in the attic for an eternity, waiting to fulfill their destiny of standing in line once more.

The boy would try not to disappoint the inanimate clutter that his dad seemed to cherish. The objects served as a medium between the two, where they could express emotion freely. They inherited the feelings of the two men, who poured themselves into the pieces of garbage on the floor. They used them as vessels to express what they couldn't. Every year that his dad refused to discard the old sleeping bag and the worn cooler was time spent thinking about his son and the memories the family shared together. It was proof he still trusted the boy, that he thought someday he could still grow up and be like him. Now the boy would carry those objects just like his dad did. He would maintain his dad's legacy through the insignificant comfort items because he had no other choice.

"These are great, Dad. Thank you so much," said the boy, who wanted to hug his dad but wasn't sure how. Instead, he desperately hoped that the tears occupying his eyelids would maintain their residency and wished he had more beer.

"You should probably be off then," said the dad blankly, seemingly not grasping the waves of emotion guiding the boy back to adolescence, back to the way things once were. "Don't wake your mom. I'll make sure to tell her you wished you could have stayed longer."

The boy was appreciative of the lie, even though it didn't make sense. He could have stayed longer without empty wishes or false remorse. He wondered if his mom would believe it more coming from her husband's mouth. Maybe he did want to stay longer, but everything seemed out of place. Maybe if he stayed long enough, everything would right itself. He thought about the time he spilled a glass of milk on a puzzle of Mount Rushmore they had worked all summer on as a family. He ran to his room and cried until the tears stopped and he just stared at the ceiling. His dad had called him back and he expected to be reprimanded, but instead, the dad dumped the rest of the pieces into the spilled milk and they merged together regardless of edge or fit.

 "Sometimes things just work themselves out," his dad had said to him, placing his steady hand on his shoulder.

After standing in the foyer for what seemed like forever, the dad pulled out his phone.

"Your mom would kill me if I didn't get a picture," he told the boy.

The boy picked up the sleeping bag and cooler and the dad fumbled with the phone, eventually allowing the boy to show him how to navigate the interface. Two men stood in the foyer of a home in northern Indiana, fulfilling an obligation they both claimed was for someone else. In actuality, behind the posturing, they were both happy that the picture was taken and relieved they had someone else to blame it on. He opened the screen door and stepped onto the front lawn, which was already buzzing with voters. The line extended far beyond their block and disappeared into the black of night. He wondered just how far the line went. For a moment he thought he saw the elderly woman with the hard candy, wishing his brother were there.

"Alright, Dad. I'll talk to you when I get done, let you know how it went," whispered the boy, with the sleeping bag under one arm and the cooler in the other hand.

He looked tired.

"See you soon," replied the dad, standing with his arms crossed.

The boy couldn't comprehend how serious the moment seemed. He anticipated some lighthearted banter but instead endured something that looked like the culmination of every decision he had made up until that point. Maybe this was redemption, maybe he'd go back to school and get out of this town, and maybe his dad knew that. That they'd see him even less after this was all over.

He left their house and began walking to find the end of the line.

He couldn't believe the types of people in line. Rabid supporters of either candidate, drunks, heroin addicts, merchants, racists, Bible thumpers, men in suits, and men in wizard hats taking shits into cans of Yankee beans. There were women holding bump stock rifles, small business owners, people who didn't appear to own anything, and doomsday preppers. Every type of person imaginable standing in line for their chance to change the trajectory of the country. It seemed more wholesome when he was a child. He looked on suspiciously as a mom and dad took turns taping telephone books to their stomachs to prevent getting shanked. There was undoubtedly an edge to the collection of freaks that turned out to vote, which far outnumbered anyone seemingly ordinary. The boy walked for five hours straight before finding the end of the line, seeing things he never thought he'd see on his way there, the most grotesque being several enormous people with Confederate flag tattoos having an orgy while a man dressed as a statue smoked meth out of a Paris Hilton fleshlight and watched intently.

He got in line behind someone who didn't look all that much different from him and was relieved that he wasn't behind the Catholic priest who slit his throat several rows up. By rule, he was still able to vote with some assistance, but the chore fell on the people behind him in line to produce his corpse at the voting station and make his selection. The boy set his cooler down, pulled a beer from it, cracked it, and began sipping. The line seemed to be moving quickly, and the boy started questioning whether he needed the sleeping bag.

"Moving pretty quick," he muttered, hoping the similar-looking voter in front of him would hear.

The man turned around briefly and stared at the boy with an expressionless face. His youthful face appeared ancient on second glance. The tip of his nose sagged into his lips, which seemed to melt into his chin. Every wrinkle was deep enough to be distinguishable even in the unlit street where they stood, the severity of their blackness conquered even the excruciating abyss of the starless South Bend evening. His eyes sank back into his face, apparently afraid of succumbing to the wrinkles that plagued the rest of him. His lips trembled and the boy could hear him clearing his throat, the productive rumble dislodging a Herculean mouth of tobacco spit and dip that dribbled slowly down the man's chin before presenting itself at the boy's feet. The log laid there provocatively, leaking saliva toward his tennis shoes and basking in the other assorted trash accumulating in the line. The boy stared at the convulsing brown mass for several seconds before looking back up at the man's glistening chin and recessed eyes. The log may as well have been a part of the man judging by his longing stare. The boy could tell he wanted desperately to put it back into his mouth, but something stopped him.

Maybe he was ready to move on from the ball of tobacco and glass shards that provided him comfort all those years, or maybe it was an offering to the boy. The hairs and demeanor of the tobacco link reminded him of a dog the family had bought when he was in third grade, but returned it days later realizing they were in over their heads.

The man reached into his trench coat and pulled out a medicinal looking brown bottle. He took a long pull from it, tilting it upwards but never breaking eye contact with the boy. He remained silent otherwise and once he had his fill, he tipped the bag toward the boy as a courtesy. The boy politely declined and retreated into the blue glow of his phone. Behind him was another normal looking man with a square haircut and wearing an ill-fitting suit, but the boy didn't risk conversation this time. He would look up from his phone every now and again and observe more brown liquid dribbling from the slackened lips of the man who had offered him a drink from his mysterious bottle. He reached into his cooler and retrieved another beer without offering any to the old man.

The line had slowed considerably after four hours and the boy bet that it was because people were giving their decision a lot of thought. He admired those who were willing to make an informed decision but grew restless. He himself had tried to do research on the candidates to pass some time, but would always be distracted by some other occurrence around him. A woman shaving her legs, a man removing a plantar wart, two men arguing over pornography preferences, insider stock trading, family recipes for the best sloppy joe, beer vendors, grilled cheeses, nitrous balloons, knife salesmen, sex offenders looking for signatures, a father and son creating a memory together, an albino giraffe being slaughtered for parts, and a group protesting animal cruelty.

The hours pounded on and he eventually grew numb to the insanity. Sometimes nothing happened at all. In those moments, it was merely a group of ordinary citizens fulfilling an undesirable but seemingly necessary obligation. Those were the worst moments. In some ways, he could comprehend the freak show more than the mundane. It was the same desire for destruction and chaos he inflicted on his body on a nightly basis. He viewed the lunatics as non-conformists and considered himself in the same realm as them even though he wasn't. They wouldn't have settled in this town, save for the sex offender, which the boy recognized as having gone to his high school.

In actuality, the boy was a manifestation of the city itself in many ways. It lived vicariously through his flesh. Born into a favorable situation and squandering it in favor of nothing. Both the city and the boy thrived on boredom and the celebration of indecision. Its yellowing hands had entered the boy long ago and now moved his limbs and mouth, convinced his mind that he was thriving, and pranced his corpse from bar to bar to the sound of a skipping jukebox. It provided heat for the spoon and guidance for the needle. It kept his strings just taut enough to discourage movement on his own, tugging them only when he felt like leaving.

His personality was binge drinking, college football, and giving up.

He reached into the cooler and pulled out another beer. He tilted from side to side in an attempt to gain a vantage point that would give him the illusion of the line moving, but no angle suggested any motion at all. The excitement of the process had dwindled with the feeling in his fingers, which grew numb in the cold early morning air. His blood vessels retreated further inwards at the smell of rain in the air. He anticipated a substantial abandonment of the line if the South Bend rain decided to fall. It was a cruel baptism in the pure misery of the city, poured by the shaky hands of a dying Catholic priest. The gray clouds looked bloated with spoiled river water and regret, eager for more victims to its undying undertow, and before the boy knew it, it was raining.

Every distended stomach from the heavens burst at once, raining freezing cold entrails onto the line, who stood defiantly against the storm. Some even cheered; it seemed to energize those who had otherwise begun to nod off. The boy envied those who were foolish enough to have hope. Visitors who had no idea how long this could last, how long it always seemed to last. Bad weather was a source of pride for the town, which was allotted four bearable days a year. Residents would make comments about shoveling global warming from their driveways for a cheap laugh from neighbors when it snowed in March.

The boy waited for the line to thin, but it didn't. He pulled the hood of his poncho tighter and was thankful for the overpriced, Notre Dame theme raincoat. He remembered purchasing the officially licensed coat and the sense of pride, knowing that he was likely partly responsible for the new solid gold altar that had been installed at the cathedral. His contribution was equivalent to the person who had died in China making the garment, who was also likely relieved that their efforts were rewarded in the form of an unnecessary solid gold church ornament.

Most of the line was woefully underdressed for the onslaught at hand, from a city that seemed to resent their presence all of a sudden. Conversation had stopped altogether, and an odd stillness set in on the once lively file of degenerates. Several more hours passed in the awful downpour. The boy looked up at the sky and pleaded with it, demanding that the clouds sew their tattered stomachs, but the rain continued on.

He reached blindly into his cooler, but his hand found nothing. The water from melted ice was indistinguishable from the rain as his pruned fingers plunged all the way to the bottom of the cooler. Looking down, he noticed there were no more beers. He was uncertain how many he had started with, but there weren't any there now. He didn't even feel drunk and yet there was nothing left to propel him. Nothing left to pass the time. Without the ability to drink, he noticed a waning interest in the day that had started with so much promise. Time didn't pass the same without the mindless consumption of domestic beer. Sometimes it seemed like if he were to stop drinking, any given moment would be preserved for an eternity. The notion of that preservation was coincidentally what he avoided and so he drank to move forward.

Another several hours passed in the punishing rain and he soaked in every single minute of it. The prospect of quitting was budding rapidly in his mind. At first, a tiny seed, its roots now pierced and wove through every pore in his brain. Once the idea of quitting was entertained, it was only a matter of time before being euthanized by the comfort it brought. The excuses and justifications subdued the will to fight. Rationalizations and promises to do better next time were slaughtered and offered as sacrifice just before retreat. The mind always quit before the body, and the boy's mind was quitting.

His shaking hands slipped his phone from his pocket and began to text his dad.

"Is any of this worth it?" he typed and sent.

"It depends on your definition of worth," replied the dad after a few minutes.

The boy looked at his phone and analyzed every word of the response. His dad always had a way of crafting statements that immediately transferred ownership back on the requester. Morsels of disappointment nestled themselves in between each letter, every word suggesting he was a failure for having sent the text at all. He plummeted into the blue light. The vagueness of it begged for interpretation and projection. It never quite said what he wanted but always ended up being what he needed or at least what he thought he needed. He was forced to stare at his own reflection as it rippled in the seven-word reply. Every word was another piece of charcoal thrown onto the turmoil furnace that raged inside of him, the smoke from its chimney polluting his blood.

What was his definition of worth? He wasn't sure anymore and actually wasn't sure if it was ever defined at all. His beliefs and emotional infrastructure were inherited from his dad, scratched into his already slight bones with lectures on accountability and whittled further by an unhealthy hunger for all-consuming guilt. Recently, he attempted to abandon that inheritance, which wasn't his to begin with. The desertion hadn't worked, and the blame stained his skin like an unhealing rash.

He decided that the message was a challenge for him to finally become his own person, that his suffering on this day would ignite the change he desired. This led him back to his decision to submit or not. He knew that if he quit now, it would be another four years of the same. Although there was a delusional superiority he routinely projected about his dull triumphs in the city that were eating him alive, part of him was aware that he had peaked, and the summit was a mountain of tick-infested mulch in a Costco parking lot. He would vote. No matter how long it took. This was his moment. His chance to have a voice.

The boy didn't text his dad back, instead deciding to sleep.

Sleeping was always a sound fallback for when the drink was out, and he'd need his energy if his vote would determine the fate of the country. Sleeping shortened the days that didn't deserve their length. It was something to do when there was nothing else. His sleeping bag was soaked, but it still provided at least one more barrier against the rain before it saturated his clothes and inevitably his bones. He wasn't quite sure how it worked for people who were sleeping, but he assumed someone would wake him once the line began to move again. He zipped himself into his bag and drifted off quickly to the dull patter of rain on his forehead.

He woke up to motion and the sound of his shirt snagging against the gravel of a dilapidated parking lot. At first slow and methodical, the pace increased rapidly as he gained consciousness. Whatever force was dragging his limp body felt an urgency in their toil that directly correlated with his grasp on reality as he woke from slumber. He frantically blinked his eyes open and sensed the ground tearing at his back, which already seemed raw and covered in varying sized lesions and lacerations. It was still raining, the drops penetrating his skull without protest. And his eyes struggled for air under the weighty eyelashes that knotted and tangled like pubic hair on the moldy tiles of his high school gym shower.

His feet were elevated slightly and appeared in the firm grasp of two enormous hands. The scarred, meat vices were created with the sole purpose of dragging. Their lengthy fingernails were caked in desperation and neglect, familiar with hardships the boy could never have imagined. Certainly capable of heating foil and fondling tar, the veins on the hands appeared blown, shattered to sand under the skin. The nails frayed further as they dug into the bones on the boy's ankles and he could feel blood pooling even in his wet pants.

Then everything stopped.

The hands released his legs as though triggered by a timer from an unknown master and they fell to the floor. The boy scrambled to his feet, feeling asphalt and broken glass pouring out of his skin into the brisk night air. Ascending with the wind before being pummeled back into the earth. The back of his clothes had vanished into the last hundred yards of asphalt, which greedily accepted the donation of licensed college football merchandise. In front of him stood the old alcoholic, another viscous strand of dip spit drainage hung from his jaw and connected to the brown bottle in his hand. Behind him was the abandoned warehouse.

They were at the front of the line and were the next two people to cast their votes. The boy considered yelling at the man, but there wasn't anything human left to comprehend human emotion. Anything the boy said would melt into the folds of the man's face, be absorbed by the wrinkles and wrung from his brown tongue into a jar containing decades of other spit, of other emotions. His eyes held a familiar indifference, similar to some of the pictures the boy saw of himself on any given bar night. Their smoothness implied decades of filing, chiseled into their state of uncaring by innumerable failures or mistakes. The glisten that suggested motion wasn't present, perhaps having evaporated into the clouds like most things did in the city. With no will to replenish the moisture and continue stirring, his pupils had grown idle and transformed to concrete.

Missing from the historic moment was the cooler. The boy cursed himself, wondering what would happen when he returned home without it. He couldn't fathom the disappointment of his dad, deprived of the joy of storing the items for another few decades.

There was a hallowed silence this close to the polling place. The boy had never experienced anything quite like it, the focus and dedication of the line was fixated entirely on the mossy, decaying wooden doors that contained the fate of every single person who had waited for their opportunity to change the world. People around him were silently praying, thumbing Rosary beads, or mumbling the National Anthem repeatedly. Some wept, still without sound, tears streamed down their faces and were patted dry with American flags. Initially embarrassed by his torn clothes, the boy saw dozens of others with the same affliction. Dragged by some other faceless dreg to where they were now. Once you entered the line, you didn't leave until you had voted. Everyone shared the same purpose in those fleeting moments, even if they voted for different people, their burden was the same. The boy understood that now.

He turned back around to an enormous green light that apparently signaled the warehouse was ready for the next voter and the ancient man in front of him limped across the now filthy red carpeting for his chance at changing everything. The boy couldn't comprehend what issues could possibly be important to the man or his capacity to physically or mentally vote. He wondered if the man would be allowed entry with the horrific spit can that seemed to spill with every staggered step. But the doors opened, just like they must have opened for every person before them. Maybe this was the beauty of it all, that even an ill-informed addict had as much say in that moment as he did. Maybe he was less different from the man than he thought. Maybe his dad wanted him to see that hope still existed in some form, no matter how dire the circumstance.

Moments later, the man stumbled back out of the doors and into the medical tent adjacent to the warehouse. Before the boy saw what was happening, the green light flashed once more, indicating that it was his turn to prove his loyalty to his country and to prove that he was willing to accept change in whatever form it came. He forgot where he was for a moment, his legs paralyzed under the pressure of decision.

His voyage was christened with the same bottle breaking as a ceremonial boat launch, as an inpatient voter behind him hurled a beer bottle at the back of his head. The glass casually shattering into the back of his skull ignited his march forward, the searing pain enough to wake him from his patriotic stupor. He turned around to see who had cast the bottle, but it didn't matter, he walked into the green light with the vigor of a one-winged moth feasting on the fading glow of an antique lamp. He didn't know what to expect, but at this point was ready for anything. As the doors opened, he began to cry. He had made it.

He walked through the corridor of the poorly lit warehouse. The first thing he noticed was the incomprehensible stench. A mixture of bouillon cubes, dried urine, and vomit marched into his nostrils like soldiers from the Revolutionary War. The moisture in the warehouse was drunk like a milkshake, his lungs burned as they spooned another heaving portion of lacteal air. He continued on despite the odor; he hadn't come this far to quit now. He would go through hell and back to fulfill what was expected of him and what he now expected of himself. After 20 seconds of walking, he saw it.

The voting booth appeared like a church confessional, complete with an American Flag beaded door. It was constructed from shoddy, unstained plywood by someone with a rudimentary understanding of carpentry from what he could tell. Several nails jutted dangerously from the structure and were caked in a substantial amount of dried blood, their reddened tips only added to the patriotic nature of the scene. He considered the likelihood that its haphazard quality was purposefully substandard to save tax dollars and ensure unbiased decisions. To the right of the booth was a small birdcage holding an enormous, deceased bald eagle.

Its broken wings were frozen between the grates of the cage, feathers scattered on the floor suggesting a brutal struggle for freedom. Whoever was in charge of feeding or caring for it had apparently forgotten. The boy considered how many other people had simply looked at the starving creature as it killed itself in the confines of the cage, or maybe it entered the cage dead and was simply something used to accent the room. He approached the structure with subdued excitement, wondering if the directions on choosing a candidate would be unveiled once he entered the glorious nationalistic womb.

His fingers swept across the beaded curtain and he was in the booth. The smell was even worse than it was in the main hall, the air somehow even thicker yet. A wooden pew sat in the middle of the tiny booth, emblazoned with several prominent alcohol brands that had apparently sponsored its construction, or the entire process.

A large neon sign also hung above the pew that read, "This changes everything" with an arrow pointing downward at its flimsy base. Although it did little to actually illuminate the surprisingly dark booth, it gave off just enough light for the boy to notice the intricacies on either wall. One side of the box was off-white and read "Democrat" while the other side was eggshell and read "Republican." Both words were in Times New Roman font and sat above what appeared to be a slightly recessed portion of the plywood. The boy took the cue from the sign and sat on the bench. The wood splintered into his bare ass and he rocked from side to side in an effort to keep the barbs from burrowing deeper.

He immediately heard the painful grinding of wood and two holes appeared in the recessed segment of the wall on either side of him. Sweat poured freely from his forehead onto the floor below, already moist with voter enthusiasm. The boy looked from side to side, wondering what would be asked of him, if he would have to dictate his decision to whomever sat on the other side. If he would be given a parchment and quill and asked to fill out a ballot like he had read about in grade school history class. Before his mind could imagine any other prospects, he heard a dull moan coming from both walls, and before he knew it, the once empty holes were now filled.

Two flaccid, uncircumcised penises breached each hole and flopped onto the wood unenthusiastically. The sound of foreskin dropping on damp lumber echoed through the enormous hall and the boy recoiled immediately. He began to stand, but before he could, a harness dropped from the top of the voting booth. It landed on his lap and fastened him in as though he were preparing to ride a roller coaster. The chewed foam roller dug into his thighs and he could smell the essence of funnel cake on the carnie contraption. He struggled briefly with it, but knew that he stood no chance against something designed by the hasty fingers of an inbred county fair employee. Even in his panic, he considered all of the efforts that had gone into making the entire experience seem authentically American. He began to think that the dead eagle in the cage outside wasn't the first of the election and certainly wouldn't be the last.

"Who will you be voting for today?" he heard a voice yawn through one of the walls, though he couldn't tell from which side.

"I'm not voting," responded the boy. "I'll be leaving as soon as you lift this goddamn thing" he continued, giving the device another futile rattle.

"Behind each wall is a Democrat candidate and a Republican candidate, and you must vote to regain your freedom," said a still indistinguishable voice. "Let this country work for you, let it save you," continued the voice.

The illusion of freedom hung sadly from either hole, sagging like a ceramic Christmas ornament on a diminutive branch on the verge of snapping. His participation in the celebration of choice and Democracy was submitting to its voluntary imprisonment. A fly landed on the Republican penis and sat rubbing its shit-covered legs in the neon luminescence before another hole opened and a hand holding a swatter pitifully swatted at the insect. It took flight briefly before landing on the Democrat penis and furiously rubbed its shit fingers once more, perhaps adding to the collection of filth in its tiny hairs. Before long, it grew bored of the endeavor and floated effortlessly through the beaded curtain and back into the long corridor. The boy was alone once more with the insufferable prospect of making a decision.

He continued to hear varying yawning and belly scratching from either wall. At some point, he smelled cheese and listened to the smacking of lips, followed by the audible licking of fingers. He could almost feel the hot tongue probing the fingernails and knuckles for any remaining cheese caught in their perspiring pores. He wanted to ask how votes were cast but he was almost certain he already knew, and his suspicion was confirmed when he noticed a small funnel duct-taped below each penis. The funnel was then stapled to a series of ribbed condoms that ran along a replica copy of the Constitution with the end of them piercing a box of limited-edition Cracker Jack. On each box of caramel-coated, molasses- soaked nuggets of sovereignty was a peeling piece of masking tape with smudged permanent marker reading "Republican Votes," and "Democrat Votes," respectively. Against the far wall was a deli meat scale that would apparently weigh the fluid of an entire country and determine which candidate had accrued more spunk and thus be the rightful heir to the free world.

"What's taking so long out there? The choice should be clear by now!" screamed the Republican candidate from behind the wall. "Which America do you want?"

Each penis remained as unmoving as ever, no visible stance on any social or economic policies that may impact the country. Each one seemed equally unaffected by the heroin epidemic plaguing the city or daily police brutalities. The bunched folds of each flaccid penis seemed content with the way things were, happily occupying the dank air of the voting booth. They appeared at home jammed through a hole in an abandoned warehouse in a crumbling city.

"Clear as day, this should be one of the easiest choices you'll ever make. You are literally molding the future for the next generation! Mold away, son!" retorted the Democrat candidate. The smell of tongue scrapings crept into the booth and stood proudly with the urine and vomit.

The boy failed to comprehend how bringing either candidate to orgasm would benefit the country, how filling a discarded box of sweetened corn kernels with cum could qualify a presidential candidate.

"Well, I guess . . . what is your stance on abortion?" the boy asked, his mind as empty as the warehouse he was trapped in.

He didn't really care but felt obligated to ask something. He didn't know any other policies, didn't know economics or foreign trade. He didn't even really understand the nuances behind the life vs. choice debate. All he knew was a video he saw in second-grade of a fetus being vacuumed from its womb and then told that it could have been the second coming of Christ. He cried for days after wondering if he had witnessed the death of his savior through a dusty VHS reel. His religion teacher had painstakingly wheeled the shared school television out of the classroom after the video and returned unimaginably sweaty. Later that day, she made the class sign a contract indicating they would never get an abortion. The ink from that contract still remained unfaded on the boy's conscience and likely on the document itself, which was undoubtedly still enshrined in the immovable gray filing cabinet behind the teacher's desk.

Maybe all he wanted was some type of answer. Any answer that could make the process incrementally more tolerable. He heard a cough from a heavily lubricated esophagus and then words cutting through a mouthful of spittle.

"I, for one, am pro the decision to choose. However, once the chooser infringes on someone else's ability to also choose, they then lose their right to become the chooser and the roles are, by law, reversed. Choosing and chooser is a fluid relationship, and I for one choose both!" said the Democrat candidate assuredly.

"I'm the exact opposite, of course! Choice should never be given unless that choice is chosen by the chooser themselves. In this case, choice is acceptable, though not encouraged. For instance, I would never contravene on a chooser's ability to choose, unless that choice was disagreeable, in which case I choose for the chooser not to choose . . . ahem . . . if that makes sense," responded the enraged Republican.

"So, which do you choose?" asked the Democrat candidate.

The boy glanced to either side at the sickening ham logs, their omnipresence made the statements even more confusing. They remained utterly stationary as if taunting the boy, their state of permanent refractory was a beacon of Democracy.

"I choose my right to not vote," said the boy, hoping that this was an option.

"Then so be it!" the two voices screamed in unison.

"You are an embarrassment to your country," said the Republican voice.

"Your grandpa died in the muck on the beaches of Normandy to allow you to sit where you are right now and choose, but I guess giving his life for his country wasn't enough for you, you privileged little fuck," chided the Democrat candidate. The once diplomatic voices were replaced with abject hatred, hissing and snarling like he had never heard before.

The boy nodded, willing to accept the shame and internalize this entire event for decades to come. The foam harness then lifted, and the boy brushed his pants off. He began to stand and placed his hand on the Republican designated wall to steady himself, his legs uneasy after what seemed like hours of inactivity. Just as his hand grazed the wall, he noticed the penis pulsate several times and belch a substantial milky discharge into the funnel below.

"Congratulations!" gasped the Republican candidate, audibly lightheaded. "You won't regret this decision! I promise to change everything or nothing at all!"

An Alvin and the Chipmunks version of the National Anthem began blaring from an ancient-sounding record player outside of the voting booth, the needle scratching and skipping over the warped wax. The celebration concluded with a wad of sopping wet confetti landing limply on the boy's head before rolling off and plopping dully on the concrete floor. Both candidates were now reciting the pledge of allegiance through blown vocal cords. He wiped what felt like adhesive from the confetti from his head and looked at the condom tubing system. The dehydrated globule labored down each segment of thinning latex, its soured yogurt threads filling each rib before spilling into the next set. It seemed to be struggling against its inevitable fate.

As the boy continued to watch the gelatinous excretion flirt with the edges of the Constitution as it slithered nonchalantly down the contraceptive maze toward the Cracker Jack box, he wondered if this was what change looked like. Maybe a stranger ejaculating into a funnel was the catalyst for a revolution. Maybe a discarded commemorative box full of cum could be the spark that ignited the great explosion.

After several painful minutes, the vote dripped sluggishly to its final resting place, merging with the thousands of other loads that were previously deposited into the disintegrating snack box. Maybe this spent seed would impregnate the box with a new savior. Someone to replace his second-grade teacher's previous messiah that had been vacuumed from its throne and now presumably ruled over a landfill kingdom of medical waste.

Something stirred within him, and he wondered if it was the feeling of being a contributing member to society, but the sound of his insides christening the floor suggested a reaction to the sadistic voting mechanism. The boy exited the booth and walked down the empty corridor toward the exit sign in the distance. He opened the door to more rain and checked his phone to see what time it was. Surprisingly the entire encounter had taken five minutes, though it had seemed like hours.

Once outside, he saw two masked surgeons beckoning him toward the medical tent that had been erected near the warehouse. One of them was waving an "I voted" cloth patch like an owner tempting their dying mutt with its favorite chew toy before executing it behind the old wooden shed in the backyard. Another stood by with a hot iron, ready to cauterize the boy's forehead with the ultimate proof of patriotism. Both sets of eyes looked bloodshot and unqualified. The iron appeared more for ironing stained Long Johns than foreheads.

The boy nodded politely and began to turn toward a weakened part in the barbed wire fence. The prospect of immense physical pain as reward for an unreciprocated and unintentional orgasm didn't seem as coveted as it once had. He remembered always wanting one of the patches as a kid.

He used to ask his mom and dad if he could feel their patches and the smooth scars surrounding it and they would politely accept. He would fall asleep listening to stories about the founding fathers and dream about a day where he could have his very own patch. Now that day was here, but the ceremony seemed like senseless branding instead of an exaltation of liberty.

Just as his fingers were about to peel back the broken links on the fence, he collapsed.

He woke up to one of the surgeons offering him a small carton of apple juice and a handful of broken animal crackers.

"You lost a lot of blood," said the surgeon grinning and giving him a nudge with his elbow.

"What happened?" asked the boy sleepily, remembering his fingers peeling the fence in their quest for actual freedom.

"That's an electric fence. You just took 20,000 volts like a champ!" said the other surgeon coming over to his hospital bed, which was just a mattress lying on the ground.

"Though that didn't cause the bleeding, that was done by this goof," said one of the surgeons, grabbing the other one and rubbing his head with his knuckle.

"Guilty as charged!" said the other surgeon, pointing at a scalpel attached to a lanyard around his neck.

"Sometimes I forget this thing is even there!" he continued, wobbling his head for comedic effect.

The boy instantly reached for his forehead, the sickening feeling of cloth forsaking his hopeful fingertips.

"Don't you worry, we went ahead and got your "I voted" melted onto your face. We even snapped this picture of you to share on Instagram if you'd like—actually you're fortunately legally obligated to. Here, have a look!" said the surgeon handing the boy his phone.

He looked at the picture they had taken. An apparent nicked artery poured blood from his neck onto the piss-stained mattress he lay on, his hair visibly burned from the electrical shock, a layer of bubbling skin hung from varying portions of the newly installed patch, and his hands had been taped into a thumbs-up position. They had even glued pennies over his shut eyelids. Their blown blood vessels enhanced the color of the copper, which added to the barely passable illusion of eyeballs.

"With a tasteful filter, I think it will generate some serious likes!" said the surgeon, helping the confused boy out of bed. He took the boy's phone and shared the picture on his Instagram with a smoothing filter and the caption, "I fucking voted!" He looked at the post for several seconds before editing the caption to include a string of indecipherable emojis.

"On your way now! Go celebrate with friends and family—today you are truly a citizen of this great country!" yelled the surgeon, cramming another handful of animal crackers into the boy's mouth and shoving him through the base of a Statue of Liberty replica that stood next to the tent.

Moments later, the boy was lying on the pavement of a familiar street. With nothing else to do, he began walking.

He walked past the few remaining people in line who stood anxiously awaiting their turn at vindication. Beyond them was the collective, malnourished bowel movement of a country. A singular, elongated skid mark on the already brimming diapers of the city.

The line, or what was left of it.

People were replaced with abandoned tents, *Good Morning America* fuck dolls, high-end yoga mats, bong water, ceremonial sacrificed animals, bibles woven from pubic hair, pumpkin spice lattes, Yankee Candles scented like marbles, and luxury coolers. He followed the line's browning intestine, ran his fingers across the sickening garbage Braille that protruded like skin tags from its membrane. Each knob or lump would eventually be scraped off and dumped into the river. After a few decades, people could hope to drink the refuse instead of having to look at it. The line itself was as parasitic as the city and both feasted on each other relentlessly, happily passing their diseases back and forth in an eternal exchange of contaminated fluids.

He used the leaking runoff that saturated the earth around it as a northern star to get home. He wasn't sure if he would stop back at his parents' house or not—he might just get in his car and leave the town forever. He couldn't imagine sitting through the celebratory dinner and cake and disappointing them again. He thought about their hopeful faces, waiting to hear how it had gone, who he had voted for, how happy he was to be an official part of the country. In some ways, he felt betrayed by them and questioned their blind allegiance to the process. He didn't understand how they could participate in something so vile election after election. Though, at a certain point, all we have is routine. Without the ability to change anything for yourself, the next best thing was stroking the cock of an anonymous lunatic in an abandoned warehouse and hoping they returned the favor at some point. Although deep down, he knew that he would always be on one side of the partition and they would always be on the other.

He wondered if this was why his brother never came back.

Before he knew it, he was in front of his parents' house. The stillness of the night air in stark contrast to how it was when he first entered the line. The only movement or sound was the rain. It was always the rain. He looked in the window where they both sat at the dining room table with a cake and balloons. He remained there for several seconds, observing their faces. His mom looked hopeful as ever and his dad checked his watch several times. They reached across the table and held each other's hands, saying nothing. The boy stood there as long as he could bear it. Eventually, his mom blew the candles of the cake out and fanned the smoke gently. His dad checked his watch once more before drawing the curtains to the house. The boy was crying again and didn't know why. For some reason, the thought of his mom waking up and relighting the candles was more painful than everything else that had happened in the last day.

Maybe he knew that he wouldn't be there to blow them out, that he would never blow them out or eat any of the cake. It would be thrown out days later, the unexceptional gesture discarded along with the hope that burned from the candles and illuminated her face. The boy would never forget the thought of the $11 sheet cake sitting in the small white trash can under their sink.

He quietly got into his car, started the ignition, and drove off. He didn't dare look back to see if the curtains had been opened to witness his departure. A small exhaust cloud remained in the place his car was parked for several seconds before disappearing into the moon.

When he got home, his roommates had already passed out drunk in front of the television, rocked to sleep by sports highlights and pills. A half-empty bottle of whiskey sat on the table along with a tipped prescription bottle that had sent its contents scrambling across the table and into the fibers of the carpet. A completely full ashtray provided the last proof he needed that it was a perfect evening. Neither one had the "I voted" patch fastened to their forehead, and he remembered a conversation about voting from several weeks earlier. Both had called it "fucking stupid," without any elaboration. Their virgin foreheads taunted the boy whose fingers instinctively pulled at a few loose fibers that hung from the patch on his forehead. The threads suggested an infuriating false hope, fragments of something that was undoubtedly permanent.

He was overcome with a vagrant jealousy, the feeling of being left behind. He remembered that tomorrow, the Notre Dame football team was playing their rival, USC. One of the biggest games of the year, which would explain their current state of jubilation. Their cares and concerns saturated their sweatpants as they lost control of their bladders in favor of total oblivion. Their mouths hung open, their skin looked pale against the dark brown cushions of the abused, over-stuffed couch, but they seemed happy. The type of resolute happiness that is unachievable without substance.

He sat on the couch and with nothing else to do but forget, he picked up several pills from the mildewy carpet and slid them into his mouth through pursed lips. He chewed them and let the bitterness engulf his tongue. He raised the bottle of whiskey and washed any remaining medicinal residue. The combination stung as it coated his empty stomach. He liked that sting. It was a familiar pain, unlike his forehead, and he knew that soon enough he would join his friends in the place they always longed to be together.

Tomorrow, they would beat the shit out of USC, and they would be responsible for that. They would recount it to each other for years to come, maybe even share the memory with their bastard kids. The school needed them; the city needed them. Without them, the city had nothing. They took their self-appointed responsibility of destroying themselves for the sake of a college football team very seriously. Tomorrow would be legendary; tomorrow would be normal, the boy thought.

He waited for his brain to liquefy and flush out of his ass and onto the floor with his two roommates, but unconsciousness didn't come like it usually did. A restlessness refused the drowning he sought, incapacitated undoubtedly, but his consciousness struggled against the water entering its lungs from the toilet it had been plunged into. Though weak, tiny bubbles still inexplicably found their way to the surface.

Frustrated, the boy had the sudden desire to masturbate, sometimes it helped him sleep. In fact, whether he'd like to admit it or not, he relied on pornography as much as liquor as a retreat from thought. The repetition of skin pounding skin functioned as a carnal metronome that was capable of injecting another dose of Novocain into his temples. He dreaded his inexorable orgasm because it meant the sound of grinding wet flesh stopped, and he was no longer drifting aimlessly and obliviously in that sea of skin. He preferred two miserable strangers fucking each other's brains out for a hundred dollars to presence in reality.

He came quickly and into the toilet bowl and looked at the disgusting mess dripping from the side and into the water. Was his wasted seed any more or less significant than either candidate? He remembered the video from second grade again and thought briefly of rescuing his messiah from the beige water but thought better of it. Instead, he decided it was better to watch it meander toward the hole where years of other unspeakable things were sent to live, a vote cast for himself. He chuckled to himself and felt his patch again as sleep began to set in.

The next day his friends stormed his room with a fresh case of beer and the energy of two people who knew a full day of drinking was ahead of them. A full day of blunders and misremembering, sexual harassment disguised as playful flirting, and physically assaulting fans of the other team for their respective allegiance. A day without consequence awaited and it would end in the same glorious fashion as the night before. Except this time, their team would be one step closer to winning it all.

The roommates wrestled with the boy for several minutes and yelled at him to stop fucking around. They danced around the room and taunted the lifeless body by singing the USC fight song. One of the roommates picked up the boy's prized Notre Dame jersey and mimicked wiping his ass with it, before accidentally vomiting up the Cheerios he had eaten with water. After several more minutes of hilarious humiliation, which also included placing their balls on the boy's forehead, one of the roommates noticed how cold the boy felt. They had never seen a dead body before, though the boy always seemed to look like this when he was extra fucked up. Never on a game day though, thought the roommate. After sitting down to a few more beers and a few lines of Adderall, the boys decided it was the right thing to do to drive him to the hospital. Maybe the doctors could revive him before game time.

They piled into the boy's car and drove to the hospital, blowing stop signs and hotboxing the old Pontiac like they always did. They took several pictures of the boy slumped in the back seat that they would hold over his head for being a total pussy when he finally woke up. When they reached the hospital, the roommates pushed the boy from the car like an old sack of McDonald's. He hit the ground just as a greasy bag would, committing fully to his resting place on the pavement. They had more important things to do than sit at the hospital with someone who couldn't handle their booze, and if they stuck around any longer, it would be impossible to get sufficiently drunk enough to enjoy the rest of the day.

Hours later, the boy was declared dead by a medical examiner. No one was quite sure why it took hours. Maybe it was just inefficiency in South Bend hospitals or the fact that there were hundreds of other bodies showing up there over the next few weeks. The doctor told his mom that it was a combination of several things, including early-onset liver failure, but the thing that pushed him over the edge was a rapidly spreading infection from the "I Voted" patch.

He consoled the boy's parents by saying that the boy likely only had a few more years to live regardless, because of the diseased liver, but it did little to take the guilt from the parents.

Notre Dame beat USC 49-21 that day and when his roommates found out that the boy died, they thought of it as the ultimate sacrifice for the team, though they ended up losing in the championship game weeks later.

They didn't care much though. They'd get it next year or the year after.

At the boy's funeral, his mom said the same thing she did about the bird all of those years ago. Holding back tears, she addressed the sparse crowd, stating that the boy died doing what he loved. In some ways, it was true.

The service was short and forgettable.

The results of the election were inconclusive according to those tallying the votes, or rather microwaving the Cracker Jack boxes full of cum and placing them on the official scale for final wcigh-ins. The weight of both candidate's output was identical. They had achieved a wholly equal number of orgasms, perfect parity.

There would be a re-vote over the next several days, and the line was already forming.

THE VERY GREAT, VERY IMPORTANT CELEBRITY COOKBOOK TRIAL

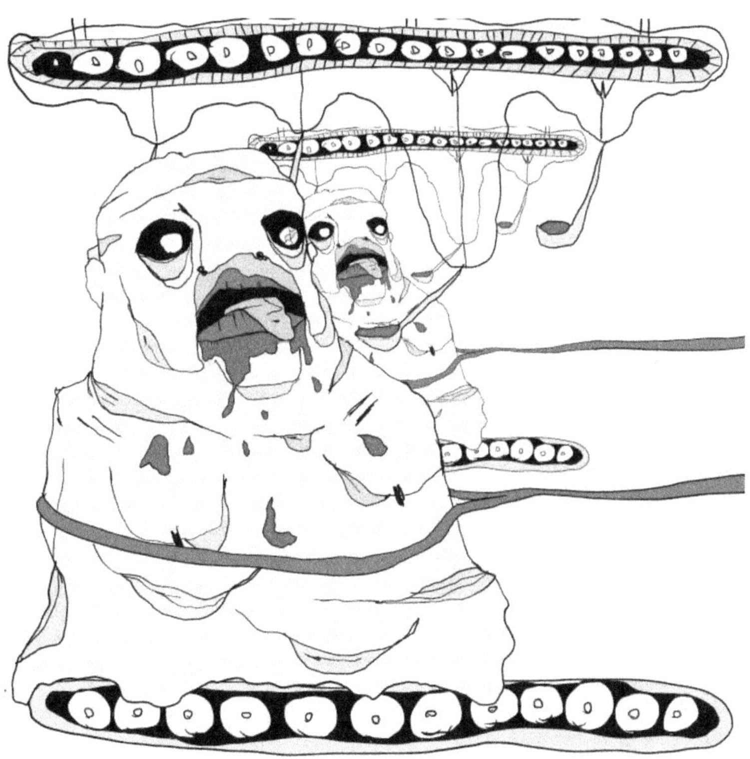

"Order! Order!" yelled an intangibly familiar looking judge to a full courtroom reaching fever pitch.

People traveled from all over the world to witness what they thought would be history. Though nowadays, the term "history" didn't carry any real significance. In fact, everything was perceived as historic in the age or eternal surveillance and corresponding consumption. It didn't take world wars or social injustices or the death of a prominent politician. Two illiterate celebrities painstakingly crafting barely comprehensible tweets while evacuating their bowels into a mid-century modern toilet would do just fine for most. In fact, it was preferred to something as boring as World War II.

Creating something memorable involved replacing blood vessels with Botox and then releasing a statement about inner beauty. It was getting liposuction, melting the jars of stinking blubber into an unaffordable, luxury porridge that provided no nutritional value and marketing it as the key to ending world hunger. It was force-feeding enough of that thinning soup into the stomachs of those willing to eat. There was always someone willing to eat and most of them didn't need any more food. They ate because there was nothing better to do and the diluted lard wasn't all that filling. It was belt sanding any distinguishing features into an unobjectionable orb and letting people rub their unblemished hands on it until climax.

The key to these historical moments wasn't quality, as the person would eventually piss the contents out with the blood from their failing kidneys. It was just making sure they were hungry enough to sip a few more spoonfuls of the rotten broth and absently convince friends and family it tasted good.

There was an impermanence to recent historical moments, a fleeting quality that bastardized them. Their deviance from traditionally defined significance grew with every year.

Adding an omnipresent stink to everything imaginable was the only way to keep the person light-headed enough to think huffing more fumes from an old gym sock was a good idea. Because memories disappeared as quickly as they were gained, it was important to keep the dampened rag over agape mouths.

This particular piece of history involved two self-proclaimed celebrity chefs sitting across from each other in a sweaty courtroom in Northern Indiana. Chrissy Montauk and Krystal Montague had a complicated past full of digital posturing that had finally climaxed in front of the world on social media. Accusations flew about their cooking and writing abilities and even though neither could cook nor write, they vehemently defended the empty brand they had constructed.

No one was quite sure how either was famous or why they had cookbooks but fame is an infallible attribute, and dutifully worshipping those who inherited the quality, regardless of method of acquisition, was viewed as an irrevocable right. It was a civic duty and considered by many to be more selfless than serving in the military. Propping up insatiable egos and lust for wealth was truly an honor unlike any other.

Followers who were equally uneducated took a break from

masturbating or contouring to lob ill-informed opinions into oblivion. They waited for replies that never came, but still felt satisfied by their contribution to nothingness. They considered the blinking cursor on their computer their spear and any trite online squabble their prized game. They considered themselves warriors and saviors.

In actuality they were the ones being hunted and slaughtered, their corpses sat in ergonomically correct desk chairs like taxidermied animals. Their limbs and faces pushed and contorted into varying positions of contentment by the celebrities they follow and products they desire to own.

Like all celebrity internet feuds, the case had been escalated to the Supreme Court and immediately took precedence over a case involving institutional racism.

Fans of either self-proclaimed chef bought tickets to the event months in advance and told friends and family about their confusing investment in something that didn't involve them at all. They prioritized manufactured celebrity outrage over all else. It seemed necessary to be there physically even though no one was paying attention. Even though the stance, their presence, and the feud itself were inconsequential at best. Nonetheless, they filled the courtroom and prepared to live-stream two talentless celebrities debate the nuances of tuna casserole to their own insufferable following. It was time and money well spent for most who cherished the opportunity to sit in a courtroom instead of the sinking coils of the La-Z-Boy chair they had just refinanced. They left their children at home and hoped their automated cat feeders would work with Cheerios.

They couldn't afford to go and couldn't afford not to go. They couldn't bear letting their heroes down. By sitting in a puddle of their own piss, like a dog waiting for an owner that would never return, they proved their worth as a human.

"Before we start the trial today, there has been a slight change in rules," said the judge, surveying the dead-looking audience.

Chrissy Montauk and Krystal Montague sneered at each other before both shitting their pants and demanding an audience member come forward to change them. Two gaunt looking men emerged from the crowd and fulfilled their destiny of sacrificing their pants for a celebrity chef. They folded the ruined pants and returned home to add them to their shrine.

A bailiff emerged from the back of the room and produced two pairs of handcuffs. He walked calmly to the two chefs and handcuffed them to the table.

"Is this really necessary?" asked Montague, the words barely making it over her massive white veneers.

"Don't you dare," said Montauk quietly, squeezing her new pair of heaving breasts together and making a duck face at the bailiff.

There was a click of handcuffs and a gasp from the crowd who all had their phones out recording every moment of the usually boring proceedings.

The judge exited his booth and placed a revolver in the

middle of the table, perfectly between the two insufferable dregs. He walked back to his elevated chair, the sound of his heavy robe dragging across the floor echoing throughout the quiet courtroom.

"There is a new standard for these trials as we realized simply a ruling one way or another wasn't enough," said the judge, stroking his chin. "No. A ruling, fine, or nebulous judgment simply cannot do any longer for a case as paramount as this."

The crowd burst into a standing ovation. Reform for meaningless celebrity altercations was something the nation had been craving for decades. Protests had recently consumed the country, furthering the apparent need for such change. They nodded to one another approvingly and mouthed, "We did this."

They wept because of the beauty of it all. They pointed at the gun and even though they didn't know what would happen with it, agreed that it was something they never thought they'd see in their lifetimes. They saw the two celebrity chefs as the last remaining hope for humanity.

"In order to determine who the real person is with a vague interest in cooking and enough plastic surgery and money to have someone else write a book for them, we'll be playing Russian roulette," said the judge, banging his gavel several more times on the desk for effect.

There were no cheers from the crowd this time.

What if it was their celebrity chef whose brains graced the floor of the courtroom? Could bone fragments and spilled blood still produce the content they needed? Could the red liquid pouring from their face be the water that filled the infinity pools they waded through? Could their shattered mouths still offer makeup tutorials or describe the uninteresting event of unboxing a mattress? Would the hole in the back of their head offer a familiar, comforting glimpse into white thong bikinis and uninformed political musings?

All of these questions plagued their minds and suffocated any sound in the room.

Chrissy Montauk and Krystal Montague were the first to shatter the oppressive silence.

"How would one of us dying qualify one or the other as the superior celebrity chef?" asked Montauk. She would have cried if she could.

"I have to say this is highly unorthodox, even by social media disputes standards," echoed Montague, perfectly timing a hair flip for a pristine boomerang opportunity.

"It's the best we could do, it was all we could do," replied the judge sullenly.

Both nodded, somehow understanding that the simple offering was their way of showing affection. They cared so deeply that someone had to die so that they could live.

Each one recognized that the opportunity to absorb the other's followers was worth horrifically dying for. Deep down, each one hoped it was them, fantasizing about future cookbook sales and an orgy of hollow remembrances following their passing. Vacant condolences and futile hashtags would help sprout the wings they needed for their perfectly curated afterlife.

The bailiff approached the table once more, put the single round in, and spun the chamber of the revolver. The clicking of the chamber spinning consumed the courtroom. When it finally stopped, he calmly handed it over to Montague and explained that because she had been the instigator, she was awarded the opportunity to go first. The logic made sense, so without much objection Montague quietly placed the gun into her mouth. Her lips engulfed the barrel completely and she held up her phone to take a pouty looking selfie.

Several members of the crowd liked the photo on Instagram immediately and agreed that she had never looked so beautiful and vulnerable. Even in a moment of potential death, the impeccable angle and filter applied to the photo was transcendent.

Her manicured fingers danced on the trigger momentarily before pulling it. There was a click and another audible exhale from the audience. Nothing. There was still hope that she would go on to create a blender shaped like her vagina or a new line of fingernail Popchips.

The bailiff retrieved the revolver and spun it once more, handing it to Montauk. She lifted the gun, but before she could place it into her mouth, a heavyset woman from the audience hurled herself over the guard rail and grabbed it. She jammed it into her enormous mouth like a spoonful of the Montauk Molten Lava Cake found in chapter nine of the book and pulled the trigger three times before it was wrestled away from her.

Deprived of her lifelong dream, of sacrificing herself for someone who was revolted by her, she lay there unmoving. The bailiff walked calmly up and beat her within an inch of her life before throwing her back into the sea of recording phones. The audience opted to not record the uninteresting beating. Bloodlust had its place in social media but not in the presence of two people whose fame was indeterminable.

He spun the gun again and handed it back to Montauk, as regardless of outcome, tributes were not allowed. She quickly put the gun to her head, which was an alternate option, and pulled the trigger. Nothing.

This continued for several hours. The revolver being passed back and forth, content being created and streamed, families gathered around their televisions to watch the culmination of everything the country stood for.

After nine hours, the judge banged his gavel on the desk.

"Bailiff, we need you to inspect the gun. One of these celebrity chefs should be dead by now," said the judge, yawning.

The bailiff walked back over to the middle of the table, both imposter chefs were pleading with their social media followers to buy more products and retweet if they agreed that they looked cute.

He lifted the gun, placed it in his own mouth and unceremoniously pulled the trigger. A boom shook the courtroom and before anyone could glance up from their phones, the bailiff's body collapsed onto the table, blood spewing from his jawless mouth. His eyes rolled into the back of his head, the pure white of them matching each of the celebrity chef's respective veneers.

The judge produced a small handkerchief and blew his nose before wiping the blood mist from his perspiring forehead.

"Case adjourned," he muttered, collecting a few papers and exiting the courtroom.

Everyone else filed out too, excited their respective chefs would keep feeding them.

A year later, two more cookbooks came out and both contained something called Bailiff Biscuit. It was a predictably underwhelming dish, but it was all anyone ate.

OUR SAVIOR WAS A SEVERED HEAD AND A BAG OF COTTON CANDY

On May 22, 2020, three enormous iron statues appeared on the boardwalk of Navy Pier in Chicago. Many perceived them as an art installation at first and then a terrorist threat and then, like everything else, as a benign inconvenience. People traveled from all over the world to worship at their feet, protest their existence and, in time, vandalize them into nothing. Various government agencies investigated the statues for days, tried to move them, and spun them as a reason to vote red or blue, depending on the ad. Religious sects scrambled to claim the symbolism as their own, with each one making a compelling case that their god had sent them as a warning to sinners and a gift to devout practitioners. They were a reason to repent, a reason to celebrate life, proof of hell and heaven and oblivion. Proof that we deserved better, or worse, or nothing at all.

Cheating husbands blamed them for ugly divorces. Pregnant women went on daytime television to claim they were the father of their unborn child. Fanatics pilgrimaged to pray there, to lay photos of deceased loved ones, to light candles with delusions of flammable miracle bait. They took acid at their feet, shot heroin, and took shits. They fucked and masturbated, fetishized, mutilated themselves, and constructed poorly made erotic shrines. Some tried to have sex with the statues themselves but were unsuccessful, unable to cum. They furiously pumped and writhed for hours and after their skin was raw enough, they returned home to cry themselves to sleep. Lotion was applied to their maimed genitalia, which were rendered useless after the inadvisable sexual conquest. Their desire to feel deprived was furthered by their own ego. They swore their dysfunction was caused by the statues and not years of repressed sexuality. Conveniently, there was always a statue to blame.

People were married and babies were baptized. Idiotic sponsored fun-runs were run. An energy drink was created to fuel the poor. A languid network television show named *Chicago Statues* premiered after *Chicago P.D.*, *Chicago Fire,* and *Chicago Transit*. The ratings were through the roof. People wept during the season finale even though it wasn't all that good. Families reunited, forgetting about whatever decade-old grievance had ripped them apart in the first place. Each one of them as unhappy as ever.

Artists were both inspired and annoyed, consumed by jealousy that someone had the idea before them even though they hadn't made anything in years. They were relieved when the statues became mainstream because it corroded the sanctity of whoever made them. It gave them the superiority they sought, claiming they could never be bought even though no one had or would ever offer. They used the term obscurity to justify their failure, heralded themselves as underground royalty to vindicate their unwanted art.

The statues were placed on currency and then removed. They were the subject of class action lawsuits and commemorated on coffee mugs and fancy socks. People claimed they bleached their chakras and broke decade-old kidney stones. A calendar holiday was created for them but was forgotten when employees found out that offices would remain open.

Priests prostituted the monuments to desperate patrons who sought salvation through spiritual commerce. Cameras were installed for 24-hour surveillance, which inevitably wound up as further beat-off material to those who craved it on Pornhub. Moms sold Xanax sand art at street fests and dads quietly resented their family there. The president awarded them a Purple Heart and then revoked it. Homeless encampments were built and burned down, set ablaze by circus clowns and the inbred carnies. Fast-casual restaurants were erected as monuments to honor their existence, and snow globes were sold at airport gift shops to forgetful moms and dads.

People attempted to take selfies with the statues, but the picture never quite turned out. Maybe it was because everyone saw something different when they looked at the colossal effigies. A wild boar head with the body of an overweight woman. Throbbing veiny breasts, a cellulite-ridden ass, and a groin covered in pubic hair so thick it was actually impossible to determine if it was a woman at all. A frail man with translucent skin eating his final bowl of soup before dying. A deep-fried chicken orgy. A Popsicle made of flies. Three impossibly muscular warriors. Gimps begging to be tortured. The 27th President William Howard Taft. People saw their moms, dads, sisters, and brothers.

Some even saw themselves in varying stages of degeneration. A baby in a hospital bed dying of dementia and a YouTube influencer eating a box of tissues. Millions reported similarly odd manifestations. At one point, there seemed to be a correlation dependent on the personality and the level of physical or mental depravity of the observer, but no one wanted to confront the possibility.

The theory was ultimately dismantled after a child saw a wooden rendering of Mickey Mouse sitting in a bathtub with a toaster, suggesting the mouse had lost its will to live.

The only similarity in something that was otherwise entirely unique was that every variation of the statue held an ancient-looking but unmistakable ax. No one seemed to question the foreboding parallel; it did not live up to their personal brand standards. Axes were neither sexy nor cute and didn't suggest in the least that the person was a wide-eyed wanderer, always ready for an adventure. It didn't feed into the perceived notion of loving to travel, or being boy crazy, or being a girl boss, or having a personality that is simply a large hat. It wasn't a kid, or a blog, or an art project, or a piece of shit pumpkin patch in Michigan. In fact, it was barely a mechanism for pointless self-promotion at all. They were initially thought to be harbingers of the next generation of social media influencers. Billboards constructed to advertise incomprehensible vanity to commuters with nothing better to do than to look. Electric paddles capable of resuscitating even the saddest digital existence. However, because the statues did not move, it made them impossible to TikTok or boomerang.

Still content was death. No one paid for art or word: They used that money for premium camera subscriptions and Angry Birds Evolution in-app purchases.

Unsurprisingly, they failed to accrue enough empty adoration to remain relevant. Everyone forgot about the statues. The blood frenzy climaxed immediately, without reciprocation and was now in a permanent refractory only to be stoked into mild arousal by an onslaught of iPhone applications. Goliath statues bestowed from possibly the heavens were now reduced to fucked-out tourist glory holes. Mocked as a sideshow barely worthy of a Segway tour led by a pear-shaped loser who loved his job.

This was before the statues changed everything.

Weeks after the statues emerged and were subsequently flushed from minds and memories into neglected rest stop toilets, the city's hospitals began to overflow. First, with pregnant women who were now weeks overdue and still unable to give birth. Gunshot victims with their jaws blown off, holding ears and fingers and handfuls of teeth. Stabbing victims with stomachs ejecting into their hands. People with strep, the flu, legendary herpes outbreaks, bacterial infections, UTIs, and every other disease under the sun. People that should be dead were not dying; those that were sick were not healing.

Conversely, those who were healthy remained as they were. Time bludgeoned forward as it always does, and in most cases, people were not even aware of the persistent, unchanging nature they were trapped in. Residents dutifully obeyed alarms and submitted assignments of little consequence to superiors, which were routinely discarded. They brushed the white sludge from their tongues and spit their dreams into toothpaste-stained sinks. The drains desperately pushed back with generic shaving cream and malnourished hair pulled from balding scalps, but the persistence behind the abandonment of hope is more powerful than human filth. People were more or less comfortable in a life void of consequences. They submitted themselves fully to a life of stagnation, settling, and blind consumption. As unmoving as the statues, they had grown to resent.

Disease experts from all over the world flew to Chicago, along with top surgeons and military police. The president and his cabinet and thousands of other self-proclaimed experts on the unprecedented, invariable physical state of residents stayed at overpriced hotels and harassed women at detestable sports bars. The city itself was quarantined, though very few people knew or cared. The prying eyes of the rest of the world feasted on the abnormalities perpetually broadcasted about the city of Chicago, unaware that they were all suffering from identical symptoms of permanence. Months bled into each other, their wounds hemorrhaged indifference and soaked into the rest of the dissolving calendar, making the passage of time an indistinguishable mess and rendering an enormous oozing scab of dates, times, and mundane obligations. Varying burdens, engagements, birthdays, doctor's appointments, and insignificant anniversaries bonded the pages of the calendar together and engorged the fibers of the dirty bandage that would someday need to be torn off.

Those who did notice were the genuinely sick, truly injured, or the aggressively pregnant.

Pregnant women begged the doctors to induce labor, who then tried with no success. Doctors attempted C-sections and their instruments bent against their skin. They were eventually released to their homes and told that on the bright side, they wouldn't have a child that would grow up to resent them or become a failure. They were assured that those were the only possible outcomes, so remaining unborn was actually the best life imaginable. Drifting vagrantly inside of a fluid pouch forever was better than most could do. Without expectation or potential, they were truly free. The uterus walls afforded them an opportunity to succeed as a parasite and minimized the impact of their inherent disappointment.

Doctors prescribed horse tranquilizers and told them to walk it off, and most took the advice and slept for hours, days, and years. They suggested that pregnant women eat spicy food, spend plenty of time crocheting baby blankets that would end up as Red Lobster butter bibs, and allow their husbands to watch football in peace. The precious clumps of cells that were supposed to rescue failing marriages across the city and become de facto personalities for people with nothing to offer refused to fulfill their involuntary obligation as savior. Lifetimes of content trapped in thousands of uteruses around the city. Some said that a divorce would surely help, but no one could be certain. Most marriages continued on with both partners consumed in silent resentment, yet neither had the courage to leave. Complacency always beats out genuine happiness in the presence of convenience. The legs and heart that used to push, to fight and feel, were being outsourced through a phone application to a middle-aged woman trying to pick out the perfect avocado in an attempt to make her rent.

Doctors couldn't operate or repair any of the people who had been in the hospital for days, though no one's condition seemed to be worsening. They remained as they were the exact moment they entered the hospital. Before long, the doctors had no other choice than to release their patients. Receptionists dutifully notified them that their insurance would not cover any of the expenses; they were offered a complimentary used hospital gown as consolation for a lifetime of medical debt.

Stab victims walked home from the hospital, hugging their gravel-coated insides and trying not to let any hot ash from their wilted cigarette fall onto the armful of pus and guts. They sat in their easy chairs and drank light beer. They waited for reruns of *America's Got Talent* to come on, vomited on themselves, contemplated their impotence, and were then rocked asleep by the fading glow of the television. Abused house animals licked at the spilled innards that had fallen unceremoniously onto the crumb-filled floor and were nonchalantly shooed away.

People with gunshot maimings dialed UberPools in an attempt to save money. They sat next to construction workers with crushed limbs and zookeepers with gonorrhea. They all enjoyed the complimentary mints, accessible cellphone charger, and the *Billboard* Top 40 music options provided by the driver, who received three stars and zero tips from each respective rider. His conversation skills were lacking, his jokes a menace to society. Most of these people never left their houses again, which was all the same for the rest of the city.

Cries from burning piss were heard regularly on quiet nights.

The government agencies, which had researched the statues for days after their arrival before hastily declaring them irrelevant junk, revisited them. Could they be something else? One acclaimed scientist attempted to insert one of the commemorative snow globes up his ass to see if it would reveal the secrets of the statues. Another smoked the wrong end of a cigarette and fondled the legs of one of the statues before walking across the street to order a soggy gyro. The president horked a sizable phlegm-forward loogie that dribbled from his chin before landing on the cracked pavement. A man in a suit scraped it up with a flimsy plastic shovel and placed it into an Altoids tin. A homeless man strangled a seagull to death a few feet away and the operator of the Ferris wheel masturbated to nothing while staring off into the abyss.

After the series of inexplicable perversions, the president looked up and noticed one other person on the entire boardwalk. He approached cautiously, wondering why or how anyone could remain on this cursed stretch of land.

A child whose face had been buried in a bowl of shrimp chowder from Bubba Gump Shrimp and had been thought to be deceased, looked up, the jaundiced porridge dripping from his tiny face. His lips quivered as a seemingly endless amount of room temperature soup continued to pour from his agape mouth. His eyes had the thousand-yard glare of a drunk capable of anything.

"Don't you realize, you spineless fucking inbreeds? These statues fucked your wives and killed your dogs. They raised skyscrapers that touched heaven and basements that touched hell. They offered you BOGO coupons to a goat-shit buffet and converted your children to Scientology. They poisoned the water and forced the chalice on anyone thirsty enough to drink from its rusted nipple. They called and you answered," he said, soup spraying everywhere on different points of emphasis throughout the statement.

The president stared at the child who slowly planted his face back into the bowl, the bubbles eventually stopping. The cryptic, almost nonsensical warning landed with profound flaccidity on the reddening ears of the president.

He walked calmly over to the child and pulled his head from the delightful appetizer. Though he had a pulse, he appeared otherwise unresponsive. He released the boy's head and it slammed heavily into the soup bowl. The bowl shattered immediately, and the soup melted slowly onto the bird shit covered floor.

A topless waitress with a pockmarked face who wore checkered roller skates dropped off a cactus-shaped postcard and bill with an implied 15 percent gratuity before retreating into the pitch-black kitchen. The sound of roller skates on the concrete floor echoed for a substantial amount of time, making everyone wonder about the depths of the kitchen. The president examined the tab, the extensiveness and quantity would suggest the child had been there for decades. A prisoner of the restaurant held hostage by affordable New American food and cheap cocktails with agonizing names.

Lt. Dan Dies Alone Whiskey Sour

Jenny's Heroin Addiction Daiquiri

Forrest Succumbs to Alcoholism Vodka Mudslide//

Handcuffed to the rotting table by his will to eat and his inability to pay. An alcoholic bastard the world surely won't miss, thought the president. He let the bill fall back into the puddle of soup being soaked into the bloated lumber. The scientist sauntered up to the mess at the table, peeled the receipt off, and casually garnished his gyro with it before sinking his gums into it and furiously tonguing it against the roof of his mouth until it mercifully tumbled down his throat.

The sound of pornography screaming in the background became too overwhelming not to notice, even competing with the revolting process of gyro digestion. The scientist and the president looked back at the Ferris wheel operator and the acclaimed scientist who had managed to fully force the snow globe into his ass despite all odds.

"He has a point," said the operator, helping himself to another fistful of Vaseline and licking a corn dog from top to bottom.

Somehow, the endorsement made perfect sense to the president and his men. The words of a masturbating idiot who had no idea how to operate a carnival ride, combined with a warning from an ancient child who was eating congealed seafood soup in a dilapidated restaurant, somehow provided an uncanny clarity.

"Everything changed when they arrived," said the president quietly, and the scientists nodded in agreement—as they always did. The scientist with the snow globe up his ass finally popped it out, which was followed by a raucous gust of unspeakable air that enthusiastically filled the room. He gazed into the skid-marked, swirling crystal ball—and at the three miniature versions of the statue that inhabited it. The rest of the room vomited and then enthusiastically gathered around the shit-obscured orb. They took turns shaking the tiny commemorative dwelling, tarnishing their hands, but hypnotized by the snow's movement and the emotionless stare of the statues. The president glanced down at his phone and checked the date that the statues appeared: May 22, 2020. He noted a calendar reminder not to kill himself along with a memo reading:

Saw ancient statues today, fucking lame. Got shit-faced with Greg after, he seems well; make sure to order an Edible Arrangement for his dead wife.

Although celebrating a friend reacquainting with alcoholism seemed like the most critical moment of the day, the statues that rendered residents of the city unable to change their physical predicament now edged out the occasion . . . slightly. The correlating timeline of hospital entrants along with the presence of the statues was unmistakable. Everyone had remained exactly as they were in the moments following the statues' arrival.

"There's nothing left to be done here," muttered the scientist, looking at his empty hands. No one in the room could determine if the statement referenced his finished gyro or the fact that three alien statues had permanently altered the concept of time and the entire nature of humanity.

The Ferris wheel operator stood silently stroking, his ears perked, but his eyes remained down. Unable to pull themselves fully from the depraved fusion of flesh before him, his turned ears suggested at least a marginal interest in the prospect of eternal life. The risk of no pornography or hastily built circus attractions in the afterlife was not a gamble he was willing to take. Though buried latent under a thick layer of empty pride and insatiable lust, he feared the humiliation when deceased friends and family discovered he was objectively a failure. A lifetime squandered doing nothing in particular. His proudest moment was impregnating a crusty sock on a nondescript Wednesday evening, saving a kid from a terrible father and the world from another generation of mediocrity.

His legacy was dipping his testicles into the communal popcorn butter and watching guests eat their own smothered bags. As far as legacies go, this surpassed what most around the world would accomplish. These statues would allow him to continue such fulfilling and glorious conquests.

The president, on the other hand, did not intend to live forever. The prospect sent his stomach tumbling and he once again retched onto the restaurant floor before walking back outside to examine the statues. He had daydreamed about the moment his bad heart finally gave out. All of his worries, anxieties, and fears exploding into oblivion in perfect harmony along with his aortic valve. He resented the valve for its resilience; it had propelled him through countless uninspired years with the same urgency as four-day-old standing bathwater. Living, but only abiding by the scientific classification of the word, he waded along with the tepid current.

After years of muling prescriptions to every part of his ailing body and mind, he imagined tired blood vessels finally succumbing to sleep. No more incessant maintenance or upkeep. Just modestly waving the white flag with what little will he had left in his hand and surrendering to the mind that had betrayed him for so many years.

The president had already begun the process of letting himself go. His fattened fingers had started loosening their grip on the precariously held rip-chord that would slow his 65-year descent into concrete. He would finally be able to slumber without the hum of his apnea machine, regular indigestion, and the nasal whine of his nagging wife. His

1,000-thread count Egyptian sheets would cease rising and falling with his labored breathing. Without the constant movement, the sophisticated bedding had a fighting chance of lasting marginally longer. He was happy to be the fertilizer that would provide potential longevity to an inanimate object. His presence, the same as a sad bowl of potato salad turning in the sun at an obligatory family picnic, could finally be discarded and eaten by broken-winged pigeons.

Dying in his sleep was the ultimate form of convenience.

He fantasized about passing quietly in the confines of a sweat-logged display bed at a Mattress Firm in northern Indiana. It would be days before one of the underpaid employees realized he was dead. He longed to fade into obscurity with the regulars who chose Mattress Firm as their preferred passing destination, and he knew that because of his celebrity, it would be almost impossible and, therefore, tempered the expectations around the glorious fantasy.

The statues stood in front of him as motionless as ever. He called the scientist over. He had to make sure his theory was correct and there was only one way to do it.

"You could be part of the biggest discovery in human history, scientist. How does that sound?" the president asked, adjusting the scientist's lab coat and brushing some dander from his sleeves.

The president put his hand on the scientist's shoulder and guided him to his knees; the scientist continued to lick furiously at his fingers attempting to extract the last morsels of gyro sweat lodged into his pores and fingernails. He sunk into the cigarette butt and broken glass gravel pit surrounding the statues, and piss began to soak the crotch of his khaki pants. He looked up at the president.

"Thank you for the shade," he muttered, referencing the president's position in regard to the sun that would otherwise be in his eyes.

The president's beady eyes fixated on the statues. The eyes of his dead son, a mistress he had fucked at a Sandals resort who later died in a drunk driving accident and a prized taxidermy buck he had killed with his late father, all stared back defiantly—or at least, it seemed that way to the president. Defiance and apathy are indiscernible. The blackness in their eyes begged him to test his theory. The colorless abyss in their sunken sockets seemed on the verge of tears, but no water fell. He waited for the tears for a moment, hoping they would help explain why they were depriving him of the death he sought, of why they were there at all. Nothing happened. Nothing ever happened. The effigies exhibited their usual infuriating tranquility.

The president pulled a revolver from his shapeless trousers and calmly planted the gun on the forehead of the scientist whose face looked as idiotic as ever, with the smell of asparagus urine filling the hot summer air. Sweat poured from the scientist's head and the barrel of the gun slipped comically off several times. The Ferris wheel operator snorted at the scene, but then demanded silence as he jammed the control lever down as he always did. The only thing he knew how to do, thrusting the empty ride through another aimless cycle.

No one had ridden the attraction in years, but he showed up anyway. Day after day, it was all he knew and all he could ever hope to know, a rotisserie of empty cars pregnant with memories that were not his. The rest of the city followed suit in their own way, pushing buttons and spinning emptiness.

The president looked at the scientist and once more at the statues, and without much pageantry, nonchalantly pulled the trigger of the gun. The bullet fell limply to the ground and all that remained was a black mark on the scientist's forehead. The marking resembled those awarded on Ash Wednesday to people seeking to prove their level of Christian devotion to friends and family who could not care less. There was otherwise nothing out of the ordinary to observe about the physical state of the scientist. His skull remained intact and his pants remained soiled. The president picked up the bullet and rolled it in his fingers like a child wielding a freshly mined wad of snot. He let it fall from his hand, allowing it to take its rightful place in the shit and garbage wedding soup that surrounded the feet of the statues.

Proof that the statues changed the trajectory of mankind disappeared into the beckoning arms of other inconsequential refuse. Though other evidence remained, the thousands of people who would never change and never die did not hold the same significance as a spent bullet from the sweaty forehead of a government employee wrestling with indigestion.

The rusted joints of the Ferris wheel screeched as it continued to turn with the hands of a masturbating lunatic, and the grating noise provided a fitting soundtrack to everything. The statues, the worship, the forgetting, the vanity, the fucking, the arson, the purgatory, and the trash all joined in a triumphant dance to the sound of a deteriorating circus ride.

The president picked up his cellphone and furiously dialed, determined to murder this scientist. To prove that the unchanging brought on by the statues was a hoax, that he could finally fulfill his destiny of shitting his pants and dying in the arms of an underpaid employee at Mattress Firm. He wanted desperately to see that bullet go through and let the world know that death was still capable. To hear the cheers around the city as a blender full of brain matter, nerve endings, and blood consecrated the worn lips of a discarded pocket pussy, the rusted crevices of an antique penny collection, and an earmarked upskirt Polaroid of a donkey dressed as a cheerleader. A scene that would capture the hearts and minds of Americans for generations to come.

Give everyone the hope he thought they needed. A restoration of reality, even if that reality meant confronting death. The opportunity to fulfill their own destinies of choking on a spoonful of cold soup while watching a limited edition true-crime series on a serial killer or a toaster slipping through their hands while trying to make a redemption brunch from the bath they hadn't left in a decade, all for a family who resented their existence.

These statues would not determine his fate or anyone else's fate, something as mystical as the concept of fate or predestination must be driven purely by impulse and an undying hunger for disposable attention. The president would restore ownership to humankind who would promptly ignore it or sell it to someone more desperate than them in an effort to get to diamond elite status in a multi-level marketing scheme. Consume it and immediately vacate it after their body pillaged what little nutrients were there. Either way, the filament illuminating their fortified lighthouses that broadcasted every thought and emotion into the indifferent night would finally pop and melt into the pitched black arteries of whatever abysmal afterlife waited.

Within ten minutes, hundreds of armed soldiers arrived at the downtrodden trash heap that was Navy Pier. The term soldier is a loose designation in this case, referring to the gun-wielding dregs that had nothing better to do on that particular day, in that particular moment. They qualified as soldiers only by way of arms and yearning for senseless destruction. Dropped off via Greyhound buses and dog sleds being pulled by hyenas. Emerging from sewer grates and characterless Irish sports bars. Parachuting from indoor skydiving establishments and helicopter tours. Sheepishly exiting varying embarrassingly themed escape rooms. Spewing from Chicago Transit cars and riding recreational vehicles. Funneling out of the revolving ring piece of mirrored office buildings. Stumbling with their pants down from a strip club with a hell of a cold cut buffet and BOGO lap dances on Tuesdays at noon. Dumping from the piss troughs at Wrigley Field with a souvenir hat they discarded peanut shells in and would someday award to their oldest son after his first DUI. They came from everywhere, in all shapes and sizes. Wearing burlap sacks and keg barrels. Allbirds shoes and Birddogs shorts. Canada Goose jackets. An elite army of witless losers.

Their personality resided comfortably in the things they

owned; their mouths were moved by lifeless conference rooms of consumer marketing teams. Their lips sewn to the hand of some sniveling, self-proclaimed product messiah who had woven the script from which they dutifully read.

They stood in a stacked horizontal line of four hundred men, some standing and some on their knees. Some facing the wrong direction entirely. Most of their weapons drawn and trained on the statues; others pointed at their own genitals. The president lumbered toward the unimpressive line of volunteers. They would function as a necessary laxative, tasked with unclogging and cleansing the world's cancerous colon. The statues operated as a brutal mechanism of constipation for humanity, which longed to fill its brimming, fetid diaper once again and bury it with a lifetime of guilt in a landfill a few blocks down from a newly christened YETI luxury cooler store. These men's knobby hands would wrestle the cork from the finest bottled vintage of human shit and let it spray freely into the agape mouths of jubilant parade attendees.

He stood behind the line and took in the afternoon air, which was as stale as ever. It entered his lungs like droplets painfully rung from the seafood-soup-soaked rug he had witnessed earlier. The air grew hotter yet, and the president looked around to determine what was causing his nausea. Every single participant of his volunteer taskforce inhaled and exhaled through their mouths. The air grazed bleeding gums and furry tongues, sat in dip spit coated stomach and lungs, and thrust back out into the world. The president raised his arm, eager to get the entire ordeal over with. He fantasized about the air conditioning units at Mattress Firm.

"On my order!" he shouted over the sound of aggressive mouth breathing and the spin of the Ferris wheel.

Hundreds of guns clicked and the sound of trembling fingers buzzed like a family of dying cicadas on a quiet summer night. The president dropped his hand and every person's fantasy of destroying something they did not understand was realized.

Bullets rained and ripped, hurtling toward the statues' skin, blowing out windows and doors, ricocheting off unsuspecting passersby. The sound of car alarms and screaming children joined the horrific churn of the wheel. Thousands of drones amassed to capture whatever was happening, unconcerned with what it was but fixated on the prospect of merely documenting and broadcasting. Some unloaded their clips faster than others, quickly reloading and pulling the trigger until their pants were soaked with ejaculate, their palms covered in gunpowder, and their brows glistening with sweat. Others pulled the trigger more methodically, taking their time and savoring the moment, their tongues wetting their flaking lips, affording the dead skin another day before falling.

Then everything stopped.

"At ease!" yelled the president, parting the enormous cloud of smoke and debris and made his way toward what he believed would be the ruins of the statues.

A single bullet careened past his head, and the sound stung his eardrum. He turned around annoyed, but every member of the volunteer army suddenly looked identical and they had begun to disperse anyways, apparently losing interest in the task at hand. They returned apathetically to their lives, unconcerned with the fate of the statues or eternal life or death after a forgettable existence. A bucket full of domestic beer, a fistful of lightly breaded pink chicken, and the potential to have an empty sexual encounter which both parties would regret were too great opportunities to miss.

Beating off to the black screen of a computer monitor that contained an obscured reflection of their sickening nude bodies before falling asleep in a king-sized bed to a batch of reheated CBS sitcoms was their revolution. This empty ritual provided them the illusion of individuality. It proved they were different. It showed that they stood for something. Like their grandfathers who fought and died in World War II, they too were dying.

The power chord to that black screen was lost years ago in a college dorm room, dropped into a puddle of bong water and drunken optimism and never recovered. There was no recharge coming, no change in scenery, no ability to choose.

The static pixels of the outdated monitor would reside in their depleted state, hopelessly willed to future generations who would inherit the same lives. Waking up and pissing an entire can of Mountain Dew Code Red into a yellowing porcelain hole while listening to a borderline celebrity covering *Imagine* by John Lennon on Vuvuzela was the only memory worth cherishing. Fighting the urge to vomit up last night's chicken alfredo Lean Cuisine dinner was a triumph worthy of telling friends and family about for weeks to come.

Their affliction was not trench foot or PTSD; it was chaffed nipples and lower back pain. Their cross to bear was not storming a beach; it was a vibration on their luxury watch, reminding them to stand more or taking daily preemptive heartburn medication. It was running out of lotion for their hands, which were slowly transforming into gnarled hooves.

The president slowed his approach when he saw the shadows, insubordinate to the hail of bullets shot by desperate psychopaths. He fell to his knees and tore at his hair, ripping out a sizable chunk and attempting to release it into the trash heap, but because of the perspiration on his hands, it matted devotedly to his flesh. He lifted his gun once more in his now hairy palm and placed the barrel in his mouth, and pulled the trigger. The bullet dropped from his mouth and rolled into the shadows of the statues. He thought for a moment one of them stirred, but it was merely a refuse cyclone caused by the propellers above. The wind raised memories from their tourist trap coffins and spun them into an apparition of pigeon droppings, McDonald's bags and party favors from an all-inclusive New Year's Eve bar deal from five years ago.

The drones hovered around him from every possible angle, capturing the moment of heartbreak and generating an untold number of likes, comments, retweets, backlash, celebration, and hatred. Most still were not sure what was going on, and would not realize it for years, but the president realized at that moment that no matter how much he wanted, nothing would ever change. He dusted his suit off, adjusted his tie, smiled, and gave the drone cameras a thumbs up. He strolled leisurely back onto the sidewalk, whistling a song he learned as a child and acting as though nothing had happened.

The scene was broadcasted, devoured, and forgotten. Shoved down in newsfeeds by the announcement of a TikTok star swallowing a keto-friendly lava lamp while dancing naked to a techno remix of an already techno remixed song. Its mouth pried open and fed cement before being drowned by the groping hands of Simon Cowell during an episode of *American Idol Rewind*. Swiped and melted into exploding gems in the latest version of Candy Crush Dementia Saga IV.

What was seen that day was taken for granted. The significance marginalized in favor of anything.

Months later, it was resurrected with memes and ironic sympathy. Social media influencers flocked to the diseased footage of the incident spilling from the carcass of another content beast as it bled out, eager to tear off a morsel to fuel their own dying brands. Diluting it with rebranding and repurposing. Making the moment theirs, even though it wasn't. Creating merchandise and smoothing filters. Doing viral dances and starting fake charities.

Though the moment itself wasn't theirs, what it proved *was*. What their final cheapened product lacked in sincerity, it made up for in relentlessness. Their stone soup ladled into fetid slop pens everywhere, pushed into veins by doctors with no medical knowledge. The omnipresent nature of their blue light discharge helped the drooling public comprehend what they could not before.

Now confronted with the supernatural, some did

everything they could to avoid it. The type of distraction obsession that can lead to madness. Countless hours spent in the confines of their own minds, constructing defense mechanisms and rationalizations, their eyes gazed upwards at the splintering rope holding the guillotine that would eventually steal their sanity. Others profited from the discovery, creating a sprawling world of new idiotic Groupon experiences to ignore.

These were attractions designated for visiting parents and people dabbling in sobriety. A diving board was installed at the top of Willis Tower. For $1,000 and a blowjob, customers could boomerang themselves plummeting into the cement below. For an extra $10, an ill-fitting T-shirt was provided with the phrase, "I tried to kill myself, but all I got was this stupid shirt," scrawled in Comic Sans coming from a text bubble attached to a cartoon rendition of the Cubs mascot, Clark the Cub.

Similar displays flooded social media feeds from around the world, peaking with a flash mob of 5,000 heavily contoured Kardashian acolytes tumbling over Niagara Falls singing the jingle from J.G. Wentworth commercials. Influencers abandoned the trend in favor of a new phone app that shipped cute pets directly to customers' doors and then returned to euthanize them days later after selfies had been posted at no additional cost. They then abandoned that trend in favor of getting pregnant and surgically attaching a GoPro camera to their unborn baby's head so that uninterested followers could experience their child's first glimpse at the world. People with nothing better to do would comment "first" and "precious" on the videos. Though there was no investment in the child, it functioned as a necessary distraction on any number of sleepless nights.

In some ways, the arrival of the statues—and what they brought with them—was the ultimate societal equalizer. They distributed unbiased eternal life and an unchanging physical state to every person, regardless of morality or economic standing. Everyone grasped the notion of living forever, but their infinite time on earth would be spent toiling away at a debt they would never pay back and watering plants that refused to grow. There was no societal collapse, no economic upheaval, no great reckoning. The rich stayed rich, the poor stayed poor, and every in-between stayed in between. An eternity of meandering and procrastination.

Endless existence meant sitting flaccidly on a toilet and waiting for a lifetime of dreams and aspirations to dump effortlessly onto a newly purchased Persian West Elm carpet. Everlasting life meant doing nothing.

It was not a new frontier; it was merely and inescapably more of the same—forever. A heaving spoonful of unscented Vaseline lubricated their mouths, readying their empty stomachs for another fistful of packing peanuts. This combination would provide the illusion of fullness for weeks. Satiating desire and granting an imaginary satisfaction to inconsequential lives everywhere.

Hundreds of years passed with predictably few technological or societal advancements. The withering legs of progress sat paralyzed underneath the weight of a skid-marked, threadbare quilt. Desire, creativity, motivation, inspiration, and any other forward momentum were suffocated by the pus leaking from engorged bedsores. People cherished their inactivity, rationalized it. Tomorrow was better than today.

Lying on the warmed sidewalk and staring directly into the sun was considered a worthy purpose for most. Others would recline in bed with an IV of Nyquil and write the next great novel in their head. Some dug unimaginably deep holes and either refused or were unable to get out. Some floated face down in piss-filled public swimming pools until lifeguards fished them out and ordered them to leave at the end of each day. They returned home in electric cars and resumed this activity in their own bathtubs while babies wailed in the kitchen. Teenagers played Russian roulette and got drunk on boxed wine.

Most abided by indecipherable orders from men in inexpensive looking antique suits, grinding of their organs, and cracking circus whips. They collected meager tips from sneering strangers in their tin cup and danced in their wooden shoes until the soles disintegrated and their feet touched the pavement.

The city of Chicago eventually decided to stop celebrating fallen soldiers on Memorial Day, and instead celebrate their own past that was not all that much different from the present. It would coincide with the day the statues arrived all those years ago. The festivities would culminate in the first running of the Chicago Marathon in 100 years. Not because anyone wanted to run, but after the human hair eating competition, pin the feather on the ostrich goiter, and an architecture tour, there was a sizable chunk of time that still required filling. The last marathon concluded with no one actually finishing the race, as participants opted instead to have a Xanax-fueled orgy followed by a virtual reality vape competition. The promoters assumed that this year would be no different; they even planned on pre-dosing the water coolers with a cocktail of prescription drugs, workout supplements, and gas station sex pills. They would set up a photo station with silly props. Mustaches and wizard hats, a grass hula skirt and a coconut bra, a strap-on dildo shaped like Steve Harvey, and a magnifying glass made of owl pellets would all contribute to curating a memorable moment. The most memorable marathon yet, in fact, which was how it was printed in Wingdings on the neon pink flyers.

Knowing that no one would complete the race, they set the finish line in the worst part of Chicago. Somewhere that very few people traveled to unless in search of an unsavory lick from the city's perspiring taint. The finish line and podium for finishers would be set in front of the three statues. Anyone unfortunate enough to finish the race would find themselves knee deep in filth at the base of the monuments that changed everything. Those interested in a post-race reception would be awarded spoiled meat, canned soup, and Sutter Home minis to hurl in the unlikely scenario someone actually decided to finish the race.

The prospect of profound humiliation woke the sleeping city and worked it into a frenzy for the upcoming festivities. It reminded some of what it was like before the statues. Imagining a single poor sap proudly crawling across the finish line only to be greeted with fiendish laughter, stabbing of fingers, and a full can of Campbell's Chunky soup directly to the face was the type of inspiration the city thrived on. Bloodlust for someone else's physical and emotional downfall was the preferred method of celebration, that much was certain. Fond memories of similar times flooded into their blood cells, piercing veins with the ease and familiarity of a heated needle. Tens of thousands of people turned up and collected the items that they hoped to shower the victor of the race with.

The Memorial Day came without much spectacle and landed on a balmy Saturday in July. The promoters surveyed the varying event locations, each place seemingly emptier than the last. Without much thought, they assumed that the prior excitement had been euthanized by the prospect of drinking a warm pint of milk and live streaming the cleaning of grime from their skin folds before falling asleep and pissing the already damp sheets until their bladders tired. Then they heard something, faint at first but grew louder as they crossed block after block toward the lake. The sound of noisemakers, laughter, guns firing into the air, and other indeterminable deliberations.

The promoters came upon a sea of people, families, friends, husbands and wives. Old and young, sick and well. All were donning the poorly designed, ill-fitting Memorial Day fun-run shirts that came complimentary with purchase of the overly expensive tickets to the event. The entirety of the city was waiting eagerly at the finish line of the marathon by the statues, forgoing any of the activities planned. Their eyes welled at the sight and upon their expected arrival, the crowd began to sing the national anthem in unanimity. The coo of 10,000 voices was heard from whoever was at the starting line to fulfill their destiny of degradation and disgrace in a downpour of assorted garbage. After the song concluded, they waited in silence, hoping that someone would come.

At the starting line stood a man in a disintegrating pinstripe suit holding a half-finished handle of off-brand, single-filtered vodka. He gazed into the sun and wiped his brow; his rubber cement sweat left the sleeve of his suit glued to his arm. He shook it violently in an attempt to dry, but his efforts were futile in the wet heat. He took an enormous pull from his bottle of hot drink, allowing the bubbles to flow upwards toward the heavens, or what he used to believe were the heavens.

Now, he didn't believe much of anything. Several hundred years prior, he was the president of the country and was laughed out of office after attempting to take his own life at the feet of the statues that the city was now celebrating. Since then, the drink primarily drove his life. He traveled the country on foot, trying to realize his dream of dying in a Mattress Firm. Staffers knew the man instantly; a black and white photo hung at every franchise, and managers gave their employees the freedom to use immediate physical force to escort him from their empty stores.

Eventually, the president returned home to Chicago and performed his disgraced moment on Michigan Avenue for leering tourists. He couldn't remember how many times he had fired that gun into his mouth. He trained raccoons that lived near his cardboard box to act as the statues. He took the second stage to the raccoons, which people often favored for pictures and tips. The tips weren't great but were usually enough to get drunk on any given day and enough to keep the raccoons marginally fed.

He wore the exact same clothes since that day, applying patches where necessary, sometimes stitching the suit to his skin to keep it from sagging into the dirt. When he read about Memorial Day, something stirred inside of him. He couldn't believe the absurdity of the celebration, something that ruined his life and changed humanity forever, distilled into a fun-run sponsored by Chase Bank. The former president knew that no one had finished a marathon in over 200 years. This would be his redemption. This would be the moment he took back from the statues. The moment would be his and his alone. A celebration stolen from those godforsaken monuments and jammed into his pockets with rusty pennies and used dental floss. He knew the emotional crusade was folly, as the statues felt nothing, but he needed this victory. He took another pull from his bottle and threw it to the ground; the glass smashed in front of the red line that he stood behind. He wondered where the other racers were, where the crowd was. He wondered who would start the race and then noticed a drone hovering in the sky with a blinking red light. Someone was watching and he figured it was as good of a time as any to kick off the festivities.

The president pulled his revolver from his trousers and fired it into the air to signify the start of the race. Then, he dropped the gun and started running. He began in a wind sprint, his arms and legs flailing uncontrollably, the drink making his heart a steel trap. His mind and limbs felt invulnerable as the vodka fueled his forward momentum. His resolve to pillage the day was unfading. After a quarter of a mile, the feeling wore off and he retched uncontrollably onto one of the steel guardrails that was placed as a crowd control mechanism for the empty streets. The spaghetti vomit hit the pavement and rolled down the hill, guiding him toward the presumptive finish line. He collapsed to his hands and knees and looked up as the drone's red light pulsated, the eye of the camera pried at his skin as it had done all of those years ago. It undressed every part of his being, saw everything that lay underneath the translucent suit. Part of him wanted to quit, walk away as he did before. There was no additional damage to be done; he could fade further into obscurity.

Maybe it was 100 years of alcoholism, maybe it was the ash that permanently stained his fingers from his sideshow revolver, maybe it was pure and utter hatred for the statues and for everyone who had mocked him into insignificance, or maybe he just had nothing better to do that day. Regardless of cause, he pushed forward, one foot after the other. At points in the 26.2 miles, his legs felt lighter than they ever had. He cherished those moments and was in awe of what his body was capable of despite what he perceived to be years of abuse and neglect. He wished those moments would go on forever. Other times he could barely move, collapsing to the pavement and using his arms to drag himself pathetically on.

Gravel ripped and tore at the suit he had worked so hard to preserve. He had no idea how much time had passed since he started the race, or how many miles he had run. All he knew was forward. More drones had gathered in the sky, some zooming in so close to his face that he could feel the breeze of their propellers blowing on his thinning hair, the heat of the red recording button. At one point, he vomited pitch black bile into the lens of a drone, which flew off immediately and disappeared into the glare of the sun. He wondered where it went; he wondered who would clean its insides and what would become of the footage. The sun came and went at least three times, from what the former president could remember, though certain sunsets may not have been sunsets at all, as he plunged in and out of consciousness.

One foot after the other, he thought. It took everything he had to perform this basic function. His body remained the same, but his mind had quit. Submitted itself to the comfort of failing again. It longed for the shade of his box, the comfort of the pathetic routine he had assembled. He swayed and crashed into one of the steel barriers, pushing it from its place on the sidewalk and creating an exit of sorts from the hellacious path of self-imposed destiny. Staring down the dark alley adjacent to the sidewalk, he imagined the smell of the dumpsters and the last fumes of a cigarette butt depositing into his lungs. He thought about the oak tree in his front yard as a child and the memories captured in its consoling shade. He remembered graduation day and mourning the death of his dad with his older brother under the enormous branches. He remembered missing the tree like a family member when he left for college and feeling like he had outgrown it when he returned.

His hands effortlessly nudged the opening farther; the barrier gates moved easier than his legs. They now glided across the pavement seamlessly. Then, he heard a sound, something different from the drone propellers' dull buzz, something human. Singing, chattering, cheering, swearing, every expressed emotion imaginable hurled into the air, summoning him back to the boiling street. He looked up and rubbed his sweat-caked eyelids furiously, not realizing until now how close to the lake he was. He stared blankly at the final mile in front of him and marveled at his ignorance. All of this time, he was running, crawling, and writhing toward the place where it all started. The place that had effectively vanquished him from civilization and beaten him into his disagreeable existence. Though he wasn't happy before the statues arrived, he never anticipated exploring the depths of sadness he had. The president hadn't returned to the actual figures since the day of the incident and didn't think he ever would. He had no reason to.

But now, the roar of the crowd grew ever more tempting. His bid for salvation mixed with an upheaval of stomach acid, which he swallowed back down. This was his day. One foot after the other. He pried himself from the cement and began the walk. He imagined showering in flowers thrown by proud onlookers. Maybe his ex-wife would be there, ready to nurse away his loneliness. Most of all, he couldn't wait to look at the statues again. Proving his worth to emotionless, inanimate statues consumed all other desires that accompanied finishing the race. His slow-moving feet picked up their gate until he reached a runner's pace. It was the best he had felt in his life. Statues or not, this was the first time he had truly felt alive.

He could see the capacity crowd packed into bleachers and stands that were constructed around the statues and a podium for the winner of the race. The noise from the crowd was reaching a fever pitch, several people had split from the main group and began running with him, holding his hands up as though he had just won a boxing match. They yelled in his ear in a language he could not comprehend and potentially did not exist. They pulled his hands and he ran faster yet. He couldn't discern what they were shouting so he turned to face one of them, expecting to see a beaming smile and a set of hopeful eyes. Instead, the face was that of featureless stone, wholly smoothed by the tedious repetition of an evaporating river. Beige in color, with holes in roughly the location a nose might be and a quivering slit that seemed too deep to comprehend. He turned to his other side and saw a similarly smoothed orb; this one had no slit at all but had sunken eyes that seemed to be blinking in Morse code. He heard the yelling again and turned to the slit, which stretched and shrank rapidly, emitting something that he interpreted as words of encouragement. He began crying at the beauty of the moment and continued running. Glory awaited. The finish line was only 100 meters away, along with the crowd that would recognize him immediately and rejoice in his accomplishment. Worship at the feet of his journey. The humanoids sprinted ahead of him, vanishing into the mass of humanity.

Two portly men in oversized white suits stood by the podium holding a crown. Their smiles looked unnatural even at this distance. Manicured with the same foreboding veneer as the welcome sign to an elitist gated suburban community. The shadows of statues helped enhance the shine of the crown, creating an altar of darkness that hoisted the glimmering object into the air like a newly baptized child. The former president had stopped running completely, taking a moment to absorb the intricacies of the scene at hand. Everything was perfect. He couldn't have curated it any better. His struggle at the start of the race would be a catalyst for future revolutions. His finish would be masturbated to by men and women alike. He would take his place among the statues as a god.

A pilled red carpet rolled slowly toward his feet, seemingly manifesting from the podium itself. Slow at first, it eventually picked up speed, skipping over pebbles, bunching, and snagging in the cracks of the poorly maintained road. It came up a few feet short of where he was actually standing, cheapening the moment with its imprecision. The former president walked three feet to the right, his feet now touching the carpet and his toes sinking into the pubic hair shag. He began to walk.

The crowd grew louder with every step toward the poorly designed 'Memorial Day' finish line advertisement. The promoters had added several racially insensitive images to the banner, maintaining that the budget-friendly iStock images somehow fitted the theme of the day. No one else seemed to notice or care. One foot after the other. Tears continued to stream down his face as he blew kisses to familiar and unfamiliar faces. He held up a single finger and raised it above his head, signifying a vague proclamation of dominance. Finally, he stood in front of the finish line tape and waited. A few seconds of showman foreplay for the crowd to become fully erect. The crowd erupted again, and a group of bleachers collapsed completely. Their cheers persevered through the destruction, which only fueled the swarm further. People spilled on top of one another, climbing and crawling, fist fighting and fucking. Everyone vied for the perfect position to heave trash on the finisher.

Not a single attendee recognized the former president; he was simply a garbage disposal that needed filling. A fucking loser volunteering as sacrifice. A spark that would ignite and burn immediately through the last shreds of kindling in an ill-fated attempt to resuscitate a dying fire. They forgot that there was a marathon preceding what was about to take place. Some forgot why they were there at all. They held their soup cans and rotten fruit tightly, hoping they wouldn't be exposed as frauds.

The former president stepped through the tape, which didn't rip but instead stuck to his clothes. He twirled clumsily and finally managed to pull the tape from its anchor. He spun around to the delight of the crowd that collectively screamed once more. Someone opened a bottle of champagne for themselves and consumed it immediately; it was as much their moment as it was his. They took a single celebratory sip, jammed the bottle up their ass, and howled in delight. Parents hugged the children they hated. The children that would never grow up, never become them.

The promoters walked over and massaged his shoulders; they cradled his head and fed him a warm energy drink. They each grabbed a forearm and guided him gently toward the podium as though he was physically incapable of navigating and stepping onto the shoddy two-inch plywood box.

"You did well; you did it very well," they said to him in unison and monotone voices as they put the cardboard crown on his head.

The former president tearfully nodded, glancing over his shoulder at the statues that appeared larger than the last time he saw them. They seemed to be leaning ever so slightly as well, but he attributed the paranoia to being without the drink. He examined them closer and they looked as unchanging as ever. Even so, he felt immense satisfaction standing before them as the entire city celebrated. He had stripped the statues of the foolish pride that he projected into their non-existent hearts, depriving them of emotions he spent decades imprinting into every fiber of their cement skin. He hoped that they too could experience shame and misery in some capacity, though deep down, he knew this was a fabrication of his imagination. The promoters turned toward the crowd; one of them produced a slender microphone from his jacket's sleeve.

"We present to you . . . the finisher of the Memorial Day marathon!" they both screamed, ripping off their suits and presenting their grotesque, fully nude bodies to the crowd.

They split the microphone in half and each consumed their respective piece, bowing to the crowd and receding behind the statues.

The former president now stood awkwardly, uncertain what to do in front of the enormous crowd. He wanted this moment so badly, and now that it was here, he was filled with regret. He decided to take one final bow and then slink off stage, take the long walk home as he did before. As he bowed, he felt something rattle his skull, seemingly detaching his brain from its stem from the forceful blow. The sting radiated from his forehead to his toes, causing them to seize and curl in terror. He stumbled backward momentarily and bent down to one knee to regain his balance. He looked onto the ground and saw a rose. He wondered how something so delicate could carry such heft, how something that required so much care could cause such devastation. He furiously rubbed the top of his head and picked up the rose, turning it over in his hand. It couldn't be. His hands were bleeding, considerably sliced by the pointed thorns of the flower stem. His skin hadn't sustained injury since the statues arrived, but now he bled. He began crying once more at the sight of the blood flowing freely from his fingertips and onto the ground. It dripped down from his extended fingers like morning dew on bent grass, first slowly dripping and then increasing its fervor and audibly pooling on the already red carpet.

The crowd fell completely silent; the man who had thrown the can of soup looked perplexedly at the former president who was now turning the rusty, shrapnel covered can over in his hands. Another can launched through the air, striking the finisher directly in the face and apparently shattering his nose, which instantly geysered red mist onto the front row of onlookers. Cheers followed the trajectory of the blood and exploded in unison with the mist. More cans now, trash of every kind rained from every direction, as did cruel laughter and crude hand gestures. The variety of filth was downright impressive, carefully chosen by the most depraved minds in the city. The unstoppable waste of the city poured onto the finisher of the marathon, drenching him in displaced grief, directionless hatred and, worst of all, Michelob Ultra bottles filled to the brim with pig shit.

Flowers galore, confetti, streamers, tinsel, champagne, lavished the former president, who was now on all fours, collapsing under the weight of adoration. He couldn't believe the generosity; he sensed a forgiveness in the crowd for what happened all of those years ago. He sensed that they longed to welcome him back into their world, that they understood and embraced his anguish. Considering all of the beautiful gifts distracted him from the escalating series of injuries plaguing his body. Concussed and with skin chewed through by broken glass and barbed wire, the former president faded toward the statues. He raised his hands thanking the crowd again for their contributions and for their lives. Dizziness set in and he sensed the world collapsing on him. Another roar from the mass, which could also sense unconsciousness settling in.

Then everything changed.

The statue that resembled his deceased son lowered the axe it was holding directly into and through his neck. It happened instantaneously, the axe split through his skin and bone with barely a sound; his body slumped before the statue, his ass unflatteringly thrust into the air. Blood spilled from the neck but was barely distinguishable after mixing with the half-eaten can of sangria baked beans that was lodged in the freshly opened neck stump. The crowd didn't notice at first, until a small shadow drifted whimsically above them. Some of the crowd pointed upwards as the head spun haphazardly through the air, and the rest reluctantly stopped throwing trash to reprimand those looking into the sky. As insults flew, so did the head, and more people looked up until the entire audience was fixated on the wobbling severed head. Hail Mary.

Eventually, it landed in the rented cotton candy machine about 40 feet away, which had served dozens of patrons throughout the day. People waited in line for hours to buy a bag of overpriced sugar insulation from a man in a melting Obama costume and a noticeable, painful appearing goiter. They laughed with each other and blushingly spent more than they could. They called it self-love. The corroded machine wrapped the head in its womb of sweetness, spinning fibers of electric blue raspberry around it with the precision and delight of a spider swaddling its final meal. Before long, the head was completely covered. Noticing the machine was done with whatever it did, the hired help scooped the candy-coated head into a plastic bag and dutifully sold it to the next customer. He greedily eyed the tip jar as he passed the makeup-stained bag over and made a comment to the child buying it about it being the heaviest bag of the day. The child and his father disregarded the plea and returned to the spectacle, which was now peculiarly silent.

"What happened?" asked the dad to his son, tossing a dirty diaper in his hand, ready to prove that he still was still capable of degrading someone. "Is it already over?"

"He's dead, it's over," replied a woman bitterly. She balled up her Memorial Day T-shirt and tossed it carelessly in the trash pile that consumed the entirety of the pier, got on an electric scooter, and rode home topless.

Most of the crowd was now fixated entirely on the corpse. The first dead person in all those years was a foreign sight to many who had forgotten what it felt like. There wasn't any real feeling, more a physical anomaly to their eyes. It wasn't sadness they felt, but surprise. About 30 seconds passed before disinterest settled in. Everyone yawned and looked at their watches, shrugged their shoulders, dropped the remaining trash they held, and began exiting the area. The promoters were nowhere to be seen and some wondered if everything they saw had been an illusion. They wondered if there would be another MemorialDay in another 100 years. They wondered if this was considered a success. Most buried whatever they felt in the moment in the blue light of their phones, happy to disregard the momentous happening in favor of blind consumption. No one would admit it, but what they buried would soon rot their core. The memory embedding itself like a tapeworm in the pit of their stomachs and devouring everything they knew.

The child was still holding the cotton candy bag; he reached in to grab a handful of the heavenly mana. His dad glanced down at the bag and saw the contented face of the man who had just died pressed against the bottom of the bag, looking at them as though they were the suicidal zoo animals at a local sanctuary. The dad swatted the piece immediately from his child's hand, grabbing the bag, and launching it as far as he could into the lake. The child cried for the rest of his life.

Months passed and people would sheepishly make offerings without friends and family knowing, seeking the same fate as the finisher. Books were written, art was made, physical feats were routinely performed, poetry read, and myriad other desperate acts. One person with no talent in particular showed the statues the social media following she had amassed. The statues refused to budge on most occasions, apparently refusing the meager sacrifices. People were left to pursue something else that would grant them freedom.

There were unlikely scenarios and occurrences where the statues would grant the person their wish and some yet where they granted death regardless of intent. No one could determine a formula and at times, it seemed to be mere proximity. They beheaded a child doodling a dinosaur chalk drawing one month and the public was left wondering why, as the drawing itself was pedestrian at best. People tried to mimic the drawing, run the same marathon the president did, but replication didn't seem to work. They spared a famous opera singer and slit the throat of someone singing shitty karaoke. The seemingly randomness of the occurrences infuriated the public, but most said nothing. They refused to advertise their pursuit. Laughed at the video recording of the president's head flying into the air. Looked at the head floating in the lake with binoculars and wondered if it would be them someday.

They toiled away at things they thought were freedom.